PUFFIN CANADA

CHIN MUSIC

GREGORY ROBERTS grew up in southern Alberta where he captained his high school football, basketball, and baseball teams. Most of his skills on the diamond have since deteriorated, but his strong arm and ninja evasiveness still allow him to be a formidable foe in a snowball fight or crabapple war.

Greg did his undergraduate work in psychology at the University of Victoria and is currently a medical student at the University of Calgary. He lives with his amazing wife, Erinn, and has learned to enjoy washing his hair with her girly shampoo.

Chin Music

by Gregory Roberts

PUFFIN
CANADA

PUFFIN CANADA

Published by the Penguin Group

Penguin Group (Canada), 90 Eglinton Avenue East, Suite 700, Toronto, Ontario, Canada
M4P 2Y3 (a division of Pearson Canada Inc.)

Penguin Group (USA) Inc., 375 Hudson Street, New York, New York 10014, U.S.A.
Penguin Books Ltd, 80 Strand, London WC2R 0RL, England
Penguin Ireland, 25 St Stephen's Green, Dublin 2, Ireland (a division of Penguin Books Ltd)
Penguin Group (Australia), 250 Camberwell Road, Camberwell, Victoria 3124, Australia
(a division of Pearson Australia Group Pty Ltd)
Penguin Books India Pvt Ltd, 11 Community Centre, Panchsheel Park,
New Delhi – 110 017, India
Penguin Group (NZ), 67 Apollo Drive, Rosedale, North Shore 0632, Auckland,
New Zealand (a division of Pearson New Zealand Ltd)
Penguin Books (South Africa) (Pty) Ltd, 24 Sturdee Avenue, Rosebank, Johannesburg 2196,
South Africa

Penguin Books Ltd, Registered Offices: 80 Strand, London WC2R 0RL, England

First published 2007

1 2 3 4 5 6 7 8 9 10   (WEB)

Copyright © Gregory Roberts, 2007

Manufactured in Canada.

ISBN-13: 978-0-14-331256-7
ISBN-10: 0-14-331256-1

Library and Archives Canada Cataloguing in Publication data available upon request

Visit the Penguin Group (Canada) website at **www.penguin.ca**

Special and corporate bulk purchase rates available; please see
www.penguin.ca/corporatesales or call 1-800-810-3104, ext. 477 or 474

To Nathan,
Who once told me in an oil truck that writing was cool

Chin Music

One

CAUGHT NAPPING—To surprise a less-than-alert runner with the result that he is picked off or suddenly caught between bases.

Contrary to what you might think, a guy won't wet his pants if you stick his finger in warm water when he's asleep. At least that was the case with six of our sleeping teammates.

I heard from my cousin Rick that the old "finger-in-warm-water" trick would have a person soaking the sheets within seven seconds—guaranteed. But, after all our efforts, there wasn't a single drop of urine on a single person's mattress. What a gyp.

We had gone to considerable effort to "borrow" the master key to the rooms at the hostel our baseball team was staying at. Basically, my best friend, Jason Parker (a.k.a. Jiggle-Me Jason), distracted the front desk attendant by rolling around on the floor doing his fake I'm-choking-on-a-ham-sandwich routine (which, incidentally was one of his career-best performances), while I snagged the key that was hanging on a hook behind the desk with a magnet taped to the end of a coat hanger. That is how it usually works; Jiggle-Me Jason comes up with the plans and takes the most treacherous roles, while I usually volunteer for the less risky responsibilities. I'm not nearly as fearless or as nutso as him.

Of all the rooms we visited, the only reaction we got came from Seth, our right fielder, who squinted his eyes at me and said, "What the . . . what the freak are you doing, ya freakin' dork head." He must have still been pretty groggy, because nobody I know calls anyone a "dork head."

After the water trick turned out to be a dud, we went to plan B. Our goal was to wreak a little havoc on Coach K., the new head coach of our high school baseball team. The K. stands for Kobrinsky, but everybody always messes it up, so he says just to call him "Coach K." According to our skip, 78 percent of people mess up his name, and another 13 percent don't try to say it. Sometimes I wonder where he gets his statistics.

So the plan was this: I was to put about a baseball-size glob of shaving cream in the sleeping Coach K.'s hand. Then the mastermind behind this scheme, Jiggle-Me Jason, would insert a blade of grass, which was strategically chosen on account of its length and its frayed end, deep into the coach's nose.

Everything went as planned when I put the shaving cream on Kobrinsky's hand. Only a faint snort. I was a bit startled, and backed up into the nightstand, causing Coach K.'s pop-bottle glasses to fall to the floor. Very lucky; now Coach could never retrieve his specs in time to see who the culprits were.

Then the good part. I gave Jiggle-Me Jason the "all clear" sign that we made up in elementary by holding my hand in a fist and flashing the pinkie finger out in two quick bursts. A goofy grin spread across Jiggle's face as he crept closer to Coach's bed, holding the blade of grass like an altar boy holds a candle. I had to plug my nose so I wouldn't laugh out loud.

I always get the hugest rush in these kinds of situations. It felt like someone opened a big package of Pop Rocks right at that spot where my ribs make an upside-down V on my stomach and they were fizzing like mad. I guess that's why I always go along with Jiggle-Me Jason's pranks. It is even more of a rush than striking someone out, or ripping a line drive up the middle to knock in a run. And that is saying something, considering I love baseball more than a hillbilly loves his banjo . . . or his sister. Baseball is basically my whole life.

At first Jiggle tickled Coach K.'s nose on the outside, but all that happened was Coach made a wheezing sound and turned his head over on the pillow. I gripped the handle of the door tighter. I don't have the *cojones* Jiggle has, I like to be close to the exit if a quick escape is necessary. Jiggle-Me Jason then tried to put the blade of grass into Coach's ear. This caused Coach K. to scratch his military flat-topped head, but with the non-cream hand. Finally Jiggle inserted the whole blade of grass deep into the inner regions of Coach K.'s schnozz. That did the trick. Coach K. sat straight up in bed and made a face like one of those cartoon characters who sniffs a pile of pepper, then he instinctively raised his hands to his face . . . it was a beautiful sight. As Coach jerked up, Jiggle dived in front of the bed in a perfectly horizontal flying position, like a guy in a war movie diving away from an enemy grenade. He even had that passionate face on like the war guys who are screaming "Noooooooooooo" in slow motion.

You know when, back in the day, people would smash a cream pie into someone's face? (I guess back then, there was no better way to insult a person.) That's what this looked like, except Coach K. smacked himself so hard with the cream that it sprayed in all directions, like a huge frothy wave when it crashes against a jagged rock. Some cream splashed onto the ceiling fan above Coach's bed, causing a shaving-cream rainstorm in the small room. A large blob flew behind him and landed in the motel heater, which produced a kind of wet-dog-bathed-in-Windex-type smell. I yanked the door open and bolted with Jiggle army-crawling on my heels, still looking passionate, like a person trying to sniff all the aroma out of a cup of coffee on TV. I looked back as I was slipping out the door and saw Coach K. fumbling around his nightstand looking for his glasses and trying to wipe the shaving cream from his eyes. There would be no way he could identify us in the morning, I thought. We both covered our mouths as we escaped outside of his room so that our laughs wouldn't incriminate us later. Through the thin walls in the hallway, we heard Kobrinsky bellow, "Ah, my nose! I think something stung me!"

We sprinted to our room like Rickey Henderson stealing second base and quietly slipped in. The door was purposely left open a crack for ease of entry. Jiggle-Me Jason used Ozzie Smith-style soft hands to close the door without a sound, and we climbed in our bed, shoes and all. We lay there for a few minutes pretending we were fast asleep, until Jiggle's leg rubbed against mine.

"Scroff, ya perv," I hissed at him. "Get that fat ham offa me." I shouldn't have said the word "fat," but it just spilled out. You should never call a fat person fat even if they're pretty cool about it like Jiggle is. It's like agreeing with someone when they say something bad about their mum—it always stings even though they may pretend it doesn't.

"Ooh, sounds like somebody's homophobic," he teased.

"No. I'm comfortable with my sexuality, dude. I just don't like your sweaty leg all weighing on me."

"Sexuality? You haven't even looked at a girl since Abby Blake puked on your shoe during hot-dog day in Grade 5. Admit it, you're just waiting to come out of the closet to make your move on the Jiggle-Meister."

"Get bent, A-hole," I said and gave him a kick in the shin. I'm not much of a swearer, but I can abbreviate with the best of them.

Jiggle then grabbed a handful of his man-boobs and kind of sung in an Irish accent, "Hey Brook, I know you want my sexy body, look at me boobies."

"You are effing disgusting." I tried to say it with a straight face, but in the end I cracked up. "Let's get some sleep; I got to rest the arm."

"Okay, see ya in the morning Elton John . . . I mean Brook."

Yeah, my name is Brook. I have gotten a lot of grief because of my feminine name over the years. Like when substitute teachers called attendance they'd be like, "Brook Gunderson, is *she* here?" Then some wise guy in the class will think it is hilarious and point to me and say, "*She's* right there," exaggerating the "she." People's jokes can be so lame sometimes. Or when I introduce myself as Brook Gunderson, the person will often say, "Nice to meet you, Brock." Then I'll have to spell it out for them, and they will say something like, "Oh Brook . . . like Brooke Shields?" And it's not like I can go by my middle name. How many cool people do you know with the name Wayburn? I swear I don't know what my parents were thinking—or smoking—when they named us kids; they named my younger sister Taylor, and me Brook. People think they got the names mixed up, or didn't look at our genders when they named us. Maybe my parents think it's funny . . . people's jokes can be so lame sometimes.

I guess I can blame my name on the '70s, the decade my parents went to college. I think the decade instilled in many people a burning desire to give their children atypical names. Apparently, during college, Dad wanted to name his sons "Led" and "Zepp."

That was in the era when my mum chose to grow hairy armpits, and Dad had long greasy hair held down by a red headband and huge earphones. My mother told me about the Zeppelin when I was lamenting the fact that my dad was such a nerd that he couldn't understand why I wouldn't wear his piano-key necktie to a formal restaurant. "He used to be cool. He used to listen to Led Zeppelin all the time," she said, thinking that one LP or eight-track or whatever could make a person cool. I saw my mum's hairy armpits with my own two eyes in an old photo of her giving the peace sign. Let me tell you, that is an image of one's mother a boy can do without. Thankfully, by the time my older brother was born, my dad had become a regular working stiff wearing a white lab coat and making rounds in the hospital. Mum had convinced my dad to abandon the name Zepp, and they settled on Frazier instead—still a bit weird. He is twenty-one, a full six years older than me, and his middle name is Wayburn too. We both inherited it from my grandpa, along with Gramps' lanky frame. That's another thing that didn't quite go our way in the gene department: Taylor got my dad's body, muscled and stocky, and my brother and I got our mum's slender frame. What did I do to deserve a cover girl's body and the name Brook?

THE HOSTEL we were staying at was pretty dingy. The bright orange curtains covering the small, barred window in our room probably matched the orange shag carpets in 1963, when the place was built. But now, the orange shag had browned to a lovely puke-orange, most noticeably on the pathway from the bed to the door. Our high school doesn't exactly break the bank on the junior boys' baseball team. Especially because this was the first trip of the year, and it was only an exhibition game against a team from Spokane.

Our coach really believed we could do well in our provincial tournament this year so he scheduled a pre-season game to sharpen us up for the regular season.

On baseball trips, Jiggle and I always work the sleeping arrangements so that he is under the sheets, and I am over the top of them with our heads at opposite ends of the bed. Hey, you might have to bunk with a guy on jayvee baseball trips, but you don't have to snuggle with him.

After about thirty minutes of lying in bed worrying that Coach K. would come barging through the faux-wood door, the Pop Rocks feeling in my stomach wore off and I got a bit drowsy. I was scheduled to pitch the next day in our first game of the season, so instead of counting sheep, I visualized how I'd work the batters with low fastballs, make them hit it on the ground, no long balls. In the moment before I dozed off I thought, "We didn't even get a knock on the door from the coach. Looks like we got away with it."

"LET ME ASSURE YOU BOYS that under no circumstances will you get away with that prank you pulled last night," bellowed Coach K. He had some toilet paper stuck up one nostril and the purple around his eyes was magnified by his thick glasses. It looked like his good eye was twitching as he spoke, but I didn't look too closely in case I started laughing. Instead, I just studied the leather of my mitt.

"Some of you might be wondering why we are all here at the diamond at 4:45 in the morning. Well, let me enlighten you. Last night one of your teammates broke into my room and assaulted me with shaving cream, then proceeded to insert a toothpick at least two inches into my nose." Coach paused to look at each of us through his good eye. I could tell he was trying to get someone to cave under the weight of the silence.

"Because I am sure that none of you will come forward to admit your guilt," he continued, "I would like the whole team to run ten foul poles, after which, somebody better come clean or it will be another ten."

"Aw crap," someone moaned.

"Whoever the morons are who creamed Coach K. they better admit it or I'm gonna knock some heads," growled our cleanup hitter, Shane Oberg.

No doubt he could do it too. Oberg is a farm boy who hits the long ball about as well as he tosses bales of hay, and he has been tossing bales on his parents' cattle farm since he was eight. He is so buff that he had to slice the sleeves on his uniform just so his biceps would get some circulation.

I decided to play dumb while I tried to think my way out of it.

"Yeah, guys," I said as I touched the sixth foul pole, "somebody has got to face the music, I ain't running no more foul poles this morning, I'm pitching tonight."

"Shut-the-freak-up, Brook," Seth said, running backward to look at me. "You freakin' woke me up last night with a cup of warm freakin' water. Of course it was you, butthead." Seth loved two things, his precious Rawlings outfielder's mitt and saying the word *freak*.

"Bite me, Seth, why don't you rub some more oil on your mitt, or something," I shouted up to Seth, and then quickly grabbed Jiggle by the sleeve.

"Dude, we gotta face the music. Seth knows, and he's going to rat us out."

"Nah, man, I can't face," replied Jiggle.

"But we gotta face, Coach K. will run us like dogs until we do."

"I can't do it. I'm not gonna face."

"You heard what Oberg said, he's going to 'knock some heads.'"

"Sorry, bro. I'm not the facing kind. Besides, you're the only one Seth can finger, I'm a free man."

"Fine, I'll tell Coach myself. I'll give him the old boys-will-be-boys speech and I'm sure he'll go easier on us than if Seth squeals."

"Do what you gotta do, bro. But as for me, I ain't faced yet and I'm not about to start," Jiggle-Me Jason said with a look of pride on his face, as if never admitting guilt was as noble as carrying your country's flag at the Olympics. I hate that unwritten rule that says you shouldn't rat out your friends. It wasn't even my idea to cream the coach. I shouldn't have to take the fall alone.

Jiggle and I were the last to meet the scowling Coach K. in front of the visiting team's dugout after jogging along the warning track from foul pole to foul pole ten times. The whole team was hunched over, breathing heavily, waiting for Kobrinsky to lay into us again.

"I hope one of you grew a conscience over the last half-hour, or you boys are in for a world of hurt."

The whole team was looking my way, all twelve of them. I was concentrating on a rock that was caught between my cleats, but I could feel their eyes on me. Why couldn't Jiggle just own up?

"Um . . . it's like this, Coach . . . sir." I spoke in a low voice and continued trying to loosen the rock stuck in my cleat. "I was really excited about our first road trip, and kinda put some shaving cream in your hand to see if you would wipe it on your face, but when the grass went up your nose you sneezed and smacked yourself so hard I got scared and ran away."

Silence . . . Somewhere on the interstate a car with a broken muffler drove by.

"I'm sorry you broke your face . . . sir."

At first I just heard a cough. Then I realized it was the type of cough you do when you're trying not to show that you're laughing.

Then I heard a couple of guys trying to keep their laughs in by breathing really loud through their noses like a machine gun. Finally, our centre fielder, Charlton Tailfeathers, who hardly ever makes a sound, busted a gut laughing. That started a chain reaction.

Everybody was killing themselves except me—I was trying to look penitent and solemn—until Coach K.'s stone face reddened and he yelled, "Gunderson, give me ten more laps, and I don't even want to see your face until the ride back to Alberta!" I was stunned. I had never seen Coach so ape-crazy before. As I put my head down and started to take my laps, Coach stung me once more. "I don't care how good a ballplayer you *think* you are, no prima donna punk will get away with that type of behaviour on my team! Consider yourself benched until further notice."

Two

BUSH LEAGUE—Describes a player who acts unprofessionally or in an unsportsmanlike manner. The term originated from the condition of unprofessional ballparks that often had bushes or shrubs in the outfield.

As I ran my ten laps, the rest of the team piled into the van and went back to the hostel to get a bit of sleep before our . . . I mean *their* five o'clock game. My chest ached with each breath, but it wasn't because I was out of wind. I felt terrible. I was mad at Coach for not being able to take a joke, I was mad at Jiggle for suggesting the idea, then not facing the music, and I was mad at myself for going along with it. This was my first season of high school baseball and I had already screwed it up.

The walk back to the hostel was cold. It wasn't even six yet and the sun was still hidden. I had forgotten to bring a jacket because Coach had woken us up so early. I had decided to jog the last five blocks when I heard a horn sound behind me. Coach K. had come up behind me in the rental van, apparently showing pity for me.

"Get in, Brook." His tone was not very understanding.

"Um, Coach . . . listen—" I wanted to explain that I wasn't a prima donna, that I was sorry, but K. cut me off.

"No, you listen. I've been coaching for twenty years and no player has ever disrespected me like that. You are in Grade 10 now—high school. It's time to grow up."

He had me there. I really wasn't very mature, or as I like to pronounce it, "ma-two-er," and some of the pranks I had been involved in weren't exactly adult.

"Coach, I'm sorry. It was just a joke."

"You see! That's the problem; everything is a joke to you. You need to check yourself, Brook, if you're gonna play on my team—and that's a big 'if'—I don't care if you are the hardest-throwing pitcher in our league, you will ride the pine until *I* think you're ready."

"But Coach . . . sir . . . I mean, baseball is *not* a joke to me." I was flustered. By threatening to keep me on the bench, Coach was taking away the only thing I had ever been good at besides making fart noises with the area behind my knee.

"I'll be the judge of that. Now get in the van."

"No thanks, Coach, I'd rather walk." I said it icy, like a TV prosecutor to the defendant. Maybe too icy.

The gears ground as he pulled back into traffic. I stood and watched my breath come out of my mouth as I exhaled in short quick bursts over and over again. I could not believe his reaction. Why was he so mad at me? All I did was put the cream in his hand; he whacked himself!

When I opened the door to our hostel room, Jiggle was sleeping like a baby. I tried to make as much noise as possible to wake him up, without actually saying "Wake up." Even though I knew that if Jiggle were in my situation he wouldn't have ratted me out, I was still mad at him.

"Wassup, Brook?" Jiggle asked, squinting through one eye.

"I could be done for the season, that's 'wassup,'" I said angrily.

"That is harsh sauce," Jiggle said, sitting up in bed. "Did Kobrinsky really say that?" There was genuine concern in his face.

"He told me that I'll 'ride the pine' until he thinks I'm serious about being a ballplayer."

"Man, I guess you'll just have to show him you're willing to do anything to get back on the roster."

"I *am* willing to do anything to get back on the roster," I said.

Jiggle thought for a moment, biting his bottom lip as he did. Finally, he said, "Okay, here's what you do. Wait until K. is cooled off a bit, then tell him you're sorry, and you want to earn his trust back, and all that bull. Then to prove it, offer to rake the infield and mow outfield once a week until the end of the season; that way he won't have to spend any of his precious budget on landscapers. I'll help you out with the mowing too."

It seemed like a pretty good plan, and I felt my neck muscles relax after he laid it out.

"I'd landscape the field, his house, and give him a foot rub every week if it meant I could get back on the mound."

EVEN THOUGH I knew I wouldn't play, I dressed for the game. I found a place at the end of the bench, after I had filled all the water bottles, put all the bats in their holders, and neatly lined the helmets on top of the dugout. I hoped Coach would notice my work.

As I sat with my chin in my hands looking out onto the field, I was grateful for the first time ever that our league only played seven innings each game instead of the traditional nine innings, like they play in the majors. I couldn't bear to watch a full nine innings.

The home team looked good. They were from Mt. Spokane High School in Mead, Washington, about a twenty-minute drive from our hostel in Spokane. The park itself was mowed nicely with bright white chalk lines extending from the batter's box through the fine clay of the infield and the dark green outfield until they reached the freshly painted yellow foul poles. It was a huge contrast to the wind-blown shale and yellow grass of our ball diamond in Lethbridge, Alberta. It was only March, and the grass back home looked like it was still suffocating from the cold, dry winter we had just had.

The other team had a few big guys in the outfield, and the pitcher warming up in the bullpen could throw hard. Their uniforms were sweet. They had dark purple vests with grey trim, and matching grey pants with a purple stripe. The pants went right down to their matching high-top cleats, and from the prominence of the logos, I guess they were sponsored by Reebok. Their fullback hats had their name stitched in the back and a large grey arrowhead with the word "Indians" on the front.

The American teams' uniforms always look better than ours do. In my town, if you don't play a game involving a rubber disc and frozen sheet of water, you can bet your Guy Lafleur rookie card that your uniforms are going to be cheapos.

Our jerseys were off-white with a red and white mustang (I learned on the internet it was a type of horse) on the chest, which had each been ironed on by the coach's wife. Our pants were white with black pinstripes. They only reached about mid-calf, and only some of us wore the stirrups that make it look okay. Some guys have red and others have black. Mine are red.

Spokane's warm-up was fast-paced and crisp. They rarely dropped a ball and all their throws were on the mark. I noticed that their catcher had a cannon for an arm. During a base-stealing situation, he caught the ball from the pitcher and, in one motion, leaned forward and gunned it to second base from his knees. The ball didn't even get higher than five feet; it looked like it was on a frozen rope until the shortstop caught it at ankle level and tagged the phantom runner.

Coach K. turned to us in the dugout and said, "Smart base running tonight, boys—12 percent of outs can be prevented with good base running."

Instead of starting on the mound, as was the plan before I got busted with the shaving cream, I helped the team take infield practice by chasing down any balls that got through. Coach K. was hitting ground balls to the infielders and yelling things like "Play's to first" and "Roll the double, boys." It was actually not exactly correct that the "boys" were going to roll the double play. Our second baseman . . . er . . . woman, was a girl. Sonya Park is about five-foot-two and has the quickest hands of anyone I have ever seen. When she was a baby, her parents immigrated to Canada from Korea, where her dad was on the national tae kwon do team. He wanted his girl to follow in his footsteps, busting blocks of wood with her head and the like, so he trained with her every day until she turned twelve. Sonya was good at tae kwon do, but five years ago, she started hockey in the winter as a goalie and led her women's team to an under-eighteen provincial championship. Her quick hands made her an outstanding butterfly goalie. The Canadian National Women's Hockey Team is hoping to get her in red and white in a couple of years.

To keep her glove hand sharp, she plays baseball with our all-guys team in the spring and summer. Although it hasn't been a picnic for us guys always waiting until she's out of earshot to let one rip, the gastrointestinal distress is worth it because she led the league in fielding percentage last year as well as bunting for base hits.

The Spokane game was only the second time the team had played outside this year. The first two months of our season were spent indoors because of the Alberta snow. We practised in the gym at the high school with tennis balls, mostly jogging to get in shape and playing catch to get our arms conditioned. I always wonder how good we would be if we could play all year round like the kids in Florida or Vegas.

There was more than the regular amount of dropped balls and overthrows in our warm-up. The guys looked a bit intimidated by the Mt. Spokane players. While we executed our infield practice, they all took a knee outside of their dugout on the third-base line, forming a perfect row. Each player down the line watched our plays intently, assessing, making mental notes of our weaknesses. They looked like a giant purple monster with fifteen spitting heads.

I don't know why everybody has got to be a tough guy at ball games. It seems that if you're an athlete, it's almost more important to show your opponent how tough you are than how well you play. I do it too when I'm pitching. I squint at the batter then spit off the mound, burning a hole in his chest with my eyes. He usually spits back, adjusts his cup, and then steps into the batter's box. A real tough-guy convention, this sport. Maybe this year I would try to be a nice guy. I could say things like "Great day for baseball, eh," or "Hope you have a good at-bat," and "It was fun pitching to you—your swing looks nice by the way."

We batted first because they were the home team. Our lead-off hitter, Charlton, watched two strikes go by, then hit a ground ball to the shortstop. He almost ran it out; it looked like he got there a split second before the throw, but the umpire called him out. He didn't even give the umpire a dirty look or say anything. Most guys would at least say "Come on!" or "Pull your head out!" but Charlton just took off his helmet and kept his eyes down.

Charlton has wheels on the base paths. He is the reigning hundred-metre dash champion of the city, and about the nicest guy you could meet. He is also a First Nations guy who moved off the reserve because his dad got a job on the city council. You always hear about First Nations people who are insulted by sports teams with names like the Redskins, the Chiefs, and the Edmonton Eskimos. They say that the teams and their logos promote stereotypes of aboriginal people, and turn important rituals into pep rallies and fanfare like the "tomahawk chop." I guess when you think about it, no other cultural minority has a team named after them. You would never see the "Toronto Asians" or the "Calgary Mexicans." I asked him if it bothered him that the team we were playing were called the Indians.

"Not really, it's sort of cool in a way, people think of our culture as powerful or something."

Our next two batters both hit pop flies, so for the first inning of our season we went three-up, three-down.

The last person on the field was our catcher. His name is Alexander but everyone just calls him Zander. He has a different ritual he does before every game—he's a bit of an odd duck. Today he touched every corner of the plate with his middle knuckle, and then licked it. Next, he stuck the Big League Chew gum that he had been chewing for exactly one hour under his left wristband, which is the last article of clothing he takes off on game day and the first to go on. Big League Chew is the only gum he uses ever since he hit a home run when he tried it the first time. If you asked him *why* he did something, he usually replied, "The baseball gods, man! You got to keep *them* on your side." When he says "them," he always rolls his eyes toward the sky. I swear he is a madman.

The first batter from Spokane was really short. He was probably five-foot-three or so, but he looked a lot smaller when he took his stance in the batter's box. He crouched over to make his strike zone about the size of a CD case. A good strategy, but kind of cheap if you ask me. Who would want to walk every time at bat? Randall, our pitcher, walked him on five pitches; the kid didn't even take the bat off his shoulder. He tried to steal second on the first pitch, but Zander threw a strike down to Sonya at second, who tagged him out easily.

The next two batters both hit grounders to Nabbi at shortstop, who threw them out easily to kill any rally hopes.

Nabbi is our best all-round athlete. He's from Zambia and moved to Canada with his aunt five years ago. He hit third in the batting order and is the only other guy on the team that's a threat to go deep other than Oberg. Our team is pretty multicultural for southern Alberta. We have one African, one Korean, one Aboriginal, and eight white guys. That's a lot of diversity considering the first time I ever saw a black person was when our family went to Disneyland for Christmas when I was eight.

In the next three innings, they scored two runs and we scored none. When the bottom of the sixth inning started, Randall was up to 120 pitches, and the score was 2 to 0. A brief flutter of hope rushed over me when Coach looked down the bench for a reliever. My eyes met his for a second, and then he looked past me to Mason, our third best pitcher.

"Get warming up then, Mason," he barked. "Warm it up good— 64 percent of injuries happen when a player isn't properly warmed up." Making up unprovable statistics is Coach K.'s way of making his comments sound more credible. It's hilarious what he comes up with sometimes. One time, when he was trying to impress us with his knowledge of the game, he told the team that "83 percent of Vikings swung their clubs like present-day major leaguers while they were pillaging villages. The other 17 percent swung their clubs like golfers. That was the genesis of baseball and golf." I have to bite my tongue sometimes when he drops those stats on us.

Mason is a shy lefty with a weird Gumby-style windup and a decent forkball. He stands about six-foot-four and is gangly like me, with feet that look too big for his body. He came in the game and got three straight fly-ball outs, one to each of the outfielders. The team jogged back to the dugout slapping hands and butts as they went. Man, I wished I could be out there. Not because of the butt slapping, but to be part of the game again.

There was a new energy in the dugout as we came up for our last at-bat. The guys were starting to chatter a bit and Seth said, "Come on, boys, it's rally-freakin'-time. Just two runs to tie."

Zander added, "Everybody turn your hats inside-out and put them on sideways . . . make sure the brims are facing east toward Yankee Stadium."

I knew it was a bit Little League style, but I didn't want to seem too good for the team, so I put my hat in rally-time position. I did not, however, join in when Seth started to sing, "Let's go rally now, everybody rally now. Rally! Ra ra rally two, three, four."

"What grade are you in, Seth?" Jiggle-Me asked. "The next thing you're gonna do is get a rubber ball and a Tee to hit off."

That shut Seth up and got a small laugh from the bench. We had the top of the order coming up for us—Charlton, Sonya, and Nabbi.

Charlton got walked, giving us a base runner with no outs. Coach K. decided on a sacrifice bunt, and Sonya laid one down the first-base line. She didn't make it to first but it did the job because Charlton ended up standing on second.

Nabbi, who was 0 for 2 so far, grabbed his 32-ounce bat and walked to the plate. He was the only player on the team who didn't use batting gloves, so his hands were calloused and hard. When he played cricket in Africa he said no one could afford gloves. He had tried them but couldn't get used to them. We all hoped he was due for a hit.

He watched a few pitches go by, waiting patiently for the one he wanted. When it came, he ripped a hanging curveball over the third baseman's head, sending the ball rolling all the way to the left-field corner. Charlton scored easy from second, and Nabbi slid headfirst into third for a triple. We were one run down with our cleanup hitter at the plate and a runner on third.

"I told you these hats would work," Zander chimed.

Oberg strode confidently to the dish. When the first pitch came down the pipe, his shoulder muscles rippled as he got good wood on it. It flew a mile high and deep into centre field. The ball didn't leave the yard, but it was deep enough for Nabbi to tag up on third after the centre fielder caught it. Tie game.

Our next batter was Jiggle-Me Jason. He has a great swing and would've probably batted cleanup for any other team in our league, but because we had Oberg, he hit fifth. He took a huge cut at the first pitch and lost his balance a bit. It looked like he was trying to hit it back to Canada.

"Take it easy, big fella," Coach K. said. "Just find a piece of grass."

He swung as hard at the next pitch as he did at the first, and caught nothing but air. On the third pitch he connected, but only on the very top of the ball. It squibbed slowly toward the pitcher and was spinning like a top. The hurler bare-handed it and tossed it to first for the third out.

"I was just giving them a false sense of security," Jiggle said to me as I brought his gear out to him. "I was saving the dinger for next at-bat." He was smiling because he knew I didn't believe his load of bull.

"Maybe next time you can hit a foul ball or something, you know, really surprise them."

The game was tied. All Mason needed to do was get three outs to go into extra innings. I could tell he was nervous. His lead foot kept landing in a different spot on the mound on his follow-through, and his pitches were all over the place. After he walked the first batter, I piped up. "Here we go kid, plant that lead foot pointing home." He didn't seem to notice my advice.

If you want to throw strikes, it is important to have a consistent pitching motion. One of the first things a coach will teach a pitcher is to point your lead foot toward where you want the ball to go. Mason was not doing it. I continued to yell advice to Mason, and he continued to pitch poorly. I was hoping that Coach K. would notice how I was being a "team player" by helping out the squad with a little constructive chatter.

The bases were loaded and Mason was feeling the pressure. After two balls in the dirt, the whole team thought he would surely walk home the winning run.

"Point your right foot toward the plate, now. You got this," I said, for about the tenth time.

"Like this?" Mason asked from the mound, sounding a bit exasperated. Then he went through his whole windup, exaggerating each movement, and planted his foot pointing toward home. The problem was, he held onto the ball.

"Balk!" the umpire yelled, and signalled the winning run to come home.

Three

GOLDEN SOMBRERO—A player who strikes out four times in one game is said to have got the Golden Sombrero.

The locker room was quiet when I kicked the door open with my spikes. Everybody was stuffing things into their bags, keeping their eyes on their own equipment. Were they blaming me for the loss? There were eleven guys who actually played who lost the game, I thought. That wasn't my fault.

"Why couldn't you just keep your pie-hole shut," spat Oberg. "Our players don't need advice from a benchwarmer with a big ego like you."

I could tell he was still miffed because I was awarded the MVP last year when he thought he should have won it. To tell the truth, I thought he should have won it too, but the team votes went in my favour. Probably because Oberg would just as soon spit in your eye as say something nice to you.

"Sorry, I was just trying to help," I stammered.

"The bases were loaded with none out," Jiggle cut in. "We lost that game before the balk."

I was glad that somebody was on my side. Good old Jiggle.

Before Oberg could say anything else, Coach K. entered the locker room to deliver the traditional post-game speech. I was happy to have everyone's eyes off me.

Jiggle sat beside me and whispered, "Get ready for the mysterious statistics."

"Ninety-seven percent of Coach's stats are invented, and 3 percent are made up," I whispered back, keeping my face dead serious.

"Besides one bad decision from our cheerleaders, you played a heck of a game tonight, Mustangs." Kobrinsky was in his tough-guy mode, doing his best impression of a coach in a made-for-TV movie about a football team from the wrong side of the tracks. "I want each of you who played tonight to know that I am proud of you. I want each of you to know that I am even more proud to be the captain of this ship." He paused to gaze at each of us through his thick glasses, which magnified his purple eye. "Seventy-eight percent of teams give up when they're losing in the last inning, but not the Mustangs of West Lethbridge High!" He let each statement resonate off the tiled shower walls. "You gave it 110 percent the whole night! When the chips were down, you fought back! That fight, my friends, is what champions are made of! We are going to take that fight, and that desire, all the way to the provincial title! Who's with me?"

Jiggle had his face buried in his first baseman's mitt so Coach wouldn't see the laugh he was trying to suppress. I normally would have found the Disney-movie style speech humorous, but today was not the day to offend Coach K. I just stared down at my socks. Coach K. is a good enough coach, but his speeches were so cheesy. Pure cheddar *fromage*.

There was silence for a few seconds. Then a slow faint clap came from the right side of the room. It slowly got louder and faster, echoing off the walls of the clubhouse. I looked over to its source and saw Seth; he was standing with a passionate look on his face and clapping his hands together like a cymbal player in an orchestra, real strong and steady. He held his hands together a little longer than normal at the end of each clap, breathing deeply through his flared nostrils. I thought a saw a lone tear roll down his cheek.

What a knot-head—he was obviously moved by the corny speech. The rest of the team was at a loss, embarrassed for Seth. Jiggle lightened the mood by clapping with him, but in a more hoedown style, complete with foot stamping. They all joined in the impromptu hoedown—anything was better than the uncomfortable silence—with a few "Yee-Haws" and "Yahoos." I gathered my stuff and slipped out as Jiggle yelled, "Do-si-do now, people."

Everyone was in a good mood as we got in the van to head back to the prairies, except me. It was already dark and we had an eight-hour drive ahead of us, so we voted to stop at a gas station to get something to eat rather than spend a few hours at a restaurant. Plus, it is always a bonus to sample the candy that we can't get up north.

Jiggle-Me was the first in the gas station and bought a large yellow Gatorade and an Oh Henry! bar before any of us even made the bell jingle on the door. With his eyebrows, he motioned me over to the public restroom.

"Dude, I had an inspiration for a sweet prank." He gets so fanatical about his plans. If he thought a quarter as much about his school work as his pranks, the guy would be an honours student. "Check it out, and lock the door."

I turned the latch on the bathroom door then watched Jiggle doing something at the main sink beside the urinal.

"Dude, if I get caught I'm a dead man! I'm bolting," I said, moving back to the door.

"Too late, bro. The damage is done—besides you weren't even involved."

"You are a sick, sick dude, Jiggle," I said when I saw what his master idea was. He had stuffed the drain with toilet paper, so no fluid could empty out, and poured the whole litre of yellow Gatorade in the sink, then floated the Oh Henry! bar in it.

"Now we enjoy the show," Jiggle said with a smirk.

We stood outside the bathroom acting as if we were looking at the fly-fishing lures and tackle boxes. I was pretending to be particularly interested in a long-brimmed hat that said, "My other hat has gone fishing." The Pop Rocks were exploding because I was worried Coach K. would bust me, but I just can't turn down an adrenaline rush.

The first guy that went into the restroom had a ponytail and was wearing a bright orange camouflage vest with his jeans tucked into his steel-toe boots. We waited about three seconds then heard, "Sweet mother of pearl, that is vulgar!" He came running out of the bathroom with a look on his face like he just swallowed a turd taco.

The next person who went in was a black guy who looked like he could be on MTV; he had nice clothes and expensive basketball shoes. His reaction almost killed Jiggle and me.

"Aw hell no! Somebody did *not* just do that in the sink!" He came rushing out of the bathroom with his face all puckered up. When he got his wits about him, he yelled to the attendant, loud enough so everyone in the gas station could hear, "You best be cleaning up your bathroom, man, 'cause somebody just up and took a dump right in your sink. And you better hurry it up too, son, 'cause that stuff is nasty!"

I laughed so hard that I had tears running down my cheeks and I think a little pee came out.

Jiggle-Me Jason kept telling everyone in the van about it on the way home. Whenever we finally stopped laughing, one of us would say, "Sweet mother of pearl, that is vulgar." We had never heard that expression before.

AFTER A FEW HOURS, everyone was pretty much asleep except Coach K. and me. I can't close my eyes in a vehicle or I'll get a bad case of motion sickness and probably hurl, and I had been rehearsing in my mind what I would say to Coach. It seemed like he was in a better mood since we played so well against the Spokane team.

"Coach, you got a second?" I whispered, as if I didn't want the sound of my voice to topple a deck of cards stacked into a castle.

"Yeah, Brook. Go ahead."

"Well, I've been thinking a lot about what you said to me at practice this morning, and I really want to apologize for how I acted. I was totally out of line." I didn't really believe it, but sometimes you just got to shovel the B.S. in the direction adults like it.

Coach K. kept his hands at ten and two on the wheel and squinted, as if he was trying to choose his words carefully. "Do you know the last time any West High baseball team played for the provincial title?"

"No sir."

"It was 1978, my senior year. We were the best in the province, probably in Western Canada, but we lost in the final by one run to the Bulldogs."

"Must have been tough," I said.

"This team is as good as the '78 team, Brook. We have a chance at going all the way; I don't want the same thing to happen again."

"What happened?" I asked.

"We had a shortstop with the best skills I had ever seen—Billy Kane. You might have heard of him, he played a little ball in the minors."

"Yeah, I've heard of him, played in Seattle, didn't he?"

"Yup. Do you know that you have the potential to be better than Billy Kane?" Coach asked.

I was surprised that Coach thought about me like that. I assumed he hated me. "Um . . . thanks," I said.

"That wasn't a compliment," he said harshly. "Potential's just a lump of coal—it isn't worth squat until the pressure makes it a diamond." Coach leaned his mouth over a coffee cup and spit a dark stream of tobacco into what I had thought was black coffee.

"Kane had the best stats in the league, and was obsessed with them. He brought a calculator into the dugout to compute his batting average after each hit. In the final game, coach gave him the sign for a sacrifice bunt to get a runner in scoring position so we could tie the game up, but he knew that a hit would put him over a .500 batting average. He ignored the coach, and hit a deep fly ball that was caught, ending our shot at the provincial title." Coach looked like he was getting steamed up again. "We lost because of a selfish prick who wanted to improve his stats. Billy Kane only did what he wanted, he didn't listen to nobody." Coach turned around in his seat and looked right at me. "I will not lose to the Northside Bulldogs again this year and more importantly, I *will not* have another Billy Kane on this team, you understand?"

"Yes sir."

Every high school has to have a nemesis. Ours was Northside High. They beat us in football and hockey, and we beat them in baseball and basketball . . . most years. Their baseball team, the Northside

Bulldogs, featured my least favourite guy on the planet, Luke Fabro. Jiggle-Me's older brother once let a live skunk loose in their gymnasium during their graduation ceremony. He got caught and had to spend a night in prison and pay a fine. He claims it was all worth it because of the legend status it gave him. They still call him "The Skunk Man" in some circles, which he thinks is pretty flattering.

We drove without speaking for a few kilometres, listening to Seth's breath whistle through his retainer that he has to wear at night. I finally got the courage up and just blurted, "I wanna mow the outfield and rake the infield once a week to prove to you that baseball isn't a joke to me."

"You're welcome to mow and rake all you want, but it will take more than that to prove to me you're serious about helping the team out. I want you to work hard, and grow up a bit, then we'll talk about putting you back in the lineup."

It was a tough pill to swallow, but at least he said I had a chance. A chance to pitch again, and maybe win the provincial championship.

We have always been a good squad. Most of us grew up playing Little League with each other, and when we were twelve-year-olds on the all-star team we almost made it to the Little League World Series in Williamsport, Pennsylvania. We lost to a team from Toronto that had a kid from the Dominican Republic who dominated us with his knuckleball. His pitches floated around in the wind and no one could hit him. The ball was coming only about half the speed that we usually saw, so our timing was way off. I think we only got four hits that whole game and they beat us 3 to 0.

I remember I cried that night on the way home. Not totally because we lost, but a combination of things, I guess. I was standing on third base in the second inning when I noticed my dad answer his cellphone in the bleachers. He was always on call, so it was no big deal, he always gets calls in the middle of my games, when he makes it to them at all, that is. But when he whispered into my mum's ear after the conversation was finished, her expression immediately changed from enjoyment to the look of somebody who just found out her house was on fire. They both left the grandstand, and my dad didn't come back until the fifth inning. My mum didn't come back at all. That was the first time my older brother Frazier had been arrested for possession of drugs. The only other major incident in our house before that happened when my mum did Frazier's laundry and found a joint in his jeans' pocket. That sent Mum and Dad into hysterics because they had a friend in college who overdosed on something that resulted in him functioning at a level just above a vegetable.

I knew something was big-time wrong when I walked, head down, toward the parking lot. My mum was sitting in the front seat of our minivan sobbing like a six-year-old girl, gasping for breath every two seconds, her voice getting raspy. The whole ride home my dad just stared at the highway. I don't think he blinked once. It was sad to see my parents so helpless, so . . . mortal. Until then, I had thought they knew all the answers. I had struck out four times that game—the Golden Sombrero—and I was only twelve, so the tears just sort of pushed on the back of my eyes till they broke through. That is how I felt now, in the van ride back to Lethbridge. I sat in the darkness and thought about how I had screwed up my favourite time of the year and ruined my relation-ship with Coach before it even started, while oncoming cars would gradually light up the inside of the van, and at the brightest point, suddenly disappear, leaving me in blackness again.

I guess that night at Little League is the reason I try to keep my nose clean. I felt so bad for my mum, like pity or something. I thought she must really love us kids because she got so bent out of shape over it all. For the first time in my life, I saw my parents as real people with feelings. I never wanted to make my mum cry like that so I promised myself I would stay out of trouble. I mean, I'm no choirboy or anything—Jiggle and I have been busted in our share of mischief—but at least that's all it was, mischief.

The hum of the tires on the pavement had everyone zonked out. Everyone but me. I couldn't sleep; I kept worrying about my future with the team. I knew I wanted to pitch, but I also knew hanging out with Jiggle and participating in his schemes was like my therapy.

As I thought about how I could still have fun with Jiggle-Me while keeping Coach happy, my train of thought was suddenly derailed. Sonya, who was sitting to my right, had shifted her weight in her sleep and her head fell on my shoulder. I froze. Every muscle in my body tensed. I couldn't really move because I didn't want to wake her up, but *man,* that was awkward. I'm not big on girls in the first place, but Sonya was my teammate, my pal. I mean, I have lost spitting contests to this girl. Besides, everybody at school thinks she is a lesbian. I haven't decided either way about the issue, but then, how would I know?

Just because Sonya plays sports and doesn't say things like "Justin Timberlake is sooo hot!" and "Don't you just totally love Pilates?" people think she is gay. Frazier said Lethbridge, which is in a cattle ranching area, is full of a bunch of livestock with small minds and the cows they make money from. He left southern Alberta as soon as he finished high school to study psychology at university in B.C. That was when I was in Grade 7. Frazier is a really smart person, but he only made it through the first semester and then had to drop out because of the dope. They didn't kick him out or anything, he just stopped going to class, stopped going to work, and stopped paying rent. The only thing he didn't stop was smoking weed. Even though my parents think he is a complete failure, to me he is still the coolest big bro around. He is one of those people that, when he tells you his opinion, you suddenly think that it was your opinion all along. One time after he came home, I started to tell him a joke. I said, "How many Indians does it take to screw in a light bulb?" I didn't even have a second to blink. He whacked me so quick and hard on the ear that I thought I would never hear out of it again.

"You think that crap is funny?" He was seething, my mellow pothead brother. A vein in his head looked like it might explode. "There are enough bigots in this world already, don't become another small-minded hick."

That was it. Frazier never hit me or gave me any more advice in my life. Well, almost never—he did tell me once never to stand behind someone who was peeing in the wind, and if you have to eat yellow snow, drain the liquid out first.

Sonya's breathing was steady and rhythmic on my shoulder. It reminded me of when I was a kid and would listen to my dad's breathing when he fell asleep watching hockey or something. I would make a game of trying to match my breaths with his; it always made me happy to be able to do something exactly the same as my dad.

My ab muscles started to relax and I felt myself drift asleep. I had no idea if Sonya was, you know, hitting from the other side of the plate, but man, her hair smelled good.

Four

SOUTHPAW—A left-handed pitcher. The original ball fields were
built with centre field aligned due east of home plate. Thus,
a left-handed pitcher's throwing hand would point south when
he stood facing the batter.

My eyelids parted a crack and I was confused about my location. It
took a few seconds to realize that I wasn't in my bedroom, but in a
fifteen-passenger rent-a-van with twelve other adolescents. The
temperature had changed as we travelled north and the windows
were all fogged up and had big droplets of water on them. Sonya
was leaning on my shoulder, I was leaning on Jiggle-Me's, and he was
leaning on the pillow he "forgot" to return to the hostel, which was
propped against the window. A drop of condensation fell on Jiggle's hat
and I almost retched thinking about the contents of the drop.

We were almost home. The sun was just a slit on the eastern
horizon as I stared out the tinted window. As we cruised on the
deserted highway, the familiar Rocky Mountains stayed motionless
in the west, while the cattle zipped by. The cows were doing what
cows do, standing, eating, lifting their tails to make cow-pies, then
standing some more.

Everyone started to wake up when we pulled into the parking lot of our high school.

Oberg said from the back of the van, "Could somebody bust open a window, it smells like a monkey's butt-crack in here."

It did smell pretty bad in the van. Everybody's breath and sweat mixed with the espresso Coach K. had been drinking to keep him awake. My mouth tasted like a kitten had used it for a litter box, so I tried to breathe more toward Jiggle than Sonya.

She woke up startled, like you would if someone just tugged on your armpit hairs.

"Wha . . . wha? Was I sleeping on you—I'm so sorry," she said. I noticed she had a sleep line imprinted on her cheek from the string of my hoody sweatshirt.

"No, it's cool," I said. "I was already asleep when you leaned on me." I lie for no reason sometimes.

"I hope I wasn't cramping your style."

"Nope, my style was officially un-cramped," I replied.

It was about four in the morning, and we all helped unload the van under the light from a street lamp. I got my stuff and threw it in the back of Jiggle-Me Jason's truck. I didn't have my driver's licence yet, being only fifteen, so Jiggle took me everywhere. Sometimes, if I had the cash, I tried to chip in for gas but Jiggle always said something like "Keep your bills, man, you can buy me a Slurpee or something." So I did. It was a great trade, I got to and from wherever I needed, and Jiggle never paid for a Slurpee.

We were about to take off when Sonya pointed to a rather large wet patch on the shoulder of my sweater.

"Oh my gosh, I think I drooled a small pond on your shoulder." I could tell she was totally embarrassed so I tried to help her out.

"Oh this? This is from a leaky water bottle I unloaded," I said.

"Shut up, Brook. You know *I* was the one doing the leaking. Just let me take it home and wash it."

I tried to protest by saying that it was no big deal but she insisted. As I was pulling it over my head, holding down my T-shirt with one hand so no one would see how skinny I was, she kind of yelped, "Eew, don't smell my drool, just hold your breath."

"I'm really sorry," she said for about the twelfth time, as I handed her the balled-up sweater.

"No problem. I heard spit was supposed to be cleaner than bottled water anyway," I replied, but I sort of doubted the words when I heard them come out of my mouth.

The brakes on Jiggle-Me's old Ford creaked as he stopped on our massive driveway. It felt eerie so early in the morning. The sun was up, but there was nothing disturbing the quiet in the cul-de-sac. No cars backing out of two-car garages, no kids on scooters, no mowers or weed whackers . . . just quiet and peace.

I punched in the code on the garage door, and the motor growled, breaking the silence of the Sunday morning as it lugged itself open. Both cars were in the garage. The eerie part wasn't the fact that the house was absolutely still—I come home to an empty house almost every day—it was the fact that I knew my *whole* family was home sleeping. It was weird to think that all five of us were in the same home, separated by the doors and walls and wall art, allowing us to occupy the same place, but be separate. I guess we're like most families—we rarely see each other. Mum and Dad both work; Mum is the artistic director for the local theatre, which takes up a lot of her evenings. She also works part-time as an instructor at the college during the day, and Dad basically lives at the hospital with his patients.

One of the advantages of having a mother who is a bigwig at the theatre is that I have never been in short supply of pirate, Peter Pan, or Shakespearian Halloween costumes. One of the major disadvantages is being forced to attend plays in which people break out into song for no apparent reason. I suppose I could handle it if people just broke into song, but what I can't handle is that everybody on the stage magically knows every word and has already mastered the intricate dance moves, complete with phoney stage smiles. When does that happen in real life? Seriously, when?

"Brooky, is that you?" It was my sister, Taylor. She had one eye closed and one squinting to see me. She was wearing a long T-shirt that came to her knees. It had a picture of a horse on it.

"Yeah, it's me. Taylor, what the heck are you doing up?"

"I heard the garage door open. Did you bring me anything from the States?"

Oops. I had forgotten that I promised my ten-year-old sister that I would bring something back for her. "Of course," I said. "You think I would forget our deal?" I reached into my pockets to see if I had anything. Nothing. Then I fished around in my baseball bag. My hand touched a half-finished package of gum. It was the best I could do. "Here you go, squirt. That is authentic made-in-USA bubble gum. I had to really pull some strings to get it."

"Wow, thanks," she said and we did our secret handshake. Bash knuckles up, bash knuckles down, then lock thumbs and flap the fingers like a bird into the sky.

"Get back to bed. We don't want to wake the rents," I said. "The Rents" was what Taylor called our parents.

She's a good kid. She can get pretty annoying, like any little sister, but we have a good system. I keep her happy by bringing her stuff when I can, and cooking her Pizza Pops and stuff after school when nobody is around, and she'll look out for me and even fib a little to my parents when I could get in trouble. Like last week when I ditched class and the principal left a message on the machine, Taylor erased it for me before Mum could hear it.

SUNDAY WAS USUALLY the morning I enjoyed a good sleep-in. That day, it lasted until the phone rang at about one in the afternoon. I answered it in an overly chipper voice, even though it woke me up. I always disguise my sleepy voice with a brighter voice than normal when the phone wakes me up. I guess I don't want the caller to feel bad, so I act like I've been up for hours. Jiggle wanted to go to the mall; he said he would eat a basket of cockroaches for a chance to get some Chinese food at the food court. I told him if he did eat the cockroaches, he would be too full to eat the sweet-and-sour pork.

"Don't be such a wise guy," he said. "I'll pick you up in ten."

"Make it twenty. I haven't showered," I told him, but he had already hung up. I splashed some water on my face just to do a little kitty wash, and then went to see if Taylor was around. I yelled her name a couple of times, but nobody was home. I like it best when nobody is around.

Jiggle picked me up after twenty minutes; I could have showered after all. Seth was sitting in the cab with him.

"Shove a cheek, geek," I said to Seth as I opened the door of Jiggle's Ford.

"No freakin' way," Seth whined. "You guys always make me sit in the freakin' middle."

"Shove a bum, chum," I said pounding my fist into my palm, mock-tough. "You know I have 'perma-shotgun' privileges in Jiggle's truck."

Seth finally conceded, letting me take the window seat, but not without a few "freak thises and freak thats" under his breath. We seem to pick on Seth a lot. We like the guy, and he is our friend, but when you pick on him, his reactions are gold. That must've been the reason why he got the butt of most of our jokes.

Seth was holding his Rawlings outfielder's glove on his lap like a rich lady holds a chihuahua. I swear he would dress that glove in a plaid sweater and booties and carry it in a purse if he could. He wanted to go to the mall because there was a shoemaker there who would brand anything you wanted on leather. Seth wanted to put the word "SOUTHPAW" on the heel of his mitt to promote his self-chosen nickname. He throws and bats left-handed, so he had decided that people should call him "Southpaw Seth." Jiggle and I refused. It is actually a cool nickname, but if people choose their own nicknames, that lessens the coolness factor. If someone told you that Earvin Johnson gave himself the title "Magic," it wouldn't be as cool, would it? That's just the kind of guy Seth is—I guess he just tries too hard.

The mall wasn't too busy, just a few junior high kids with overly baggy pants and spiky hair. The boys were mostly shorter than the girls and the girls were all wearing white skate-shoes and tight jeans. I bet not a single one of them could ride a skateboard.

Jiggle was on a mission to get to Fresh Choy's and carved a straight line to the counter. He ordered the choose-any-three-with-rice combo and I went for the any-two. I had a feeling I would get sick after this meal, like every time I buy from the food court, but it looked so good I just had to have it. Seth said he wasn't hungry, and then speed-walked in the direction of the shoemaker, barely able to hide his giddiness. We sat at a table after getting our food, and Jiggle inhaled his ginger beef, but left the rice. Between bites, he told me about his plan for the afternoon.

"All I need is a loonie," he said through a mouthful. "You don't have a loonie on you, do ya?"

"I think I do, but what are you going to do with it?"

"You'll see, Brooky my boy. You'll see."

After we wolfed down our food, and I started to feel a stomach ache coming on, we walked out of the mall, through some mall-rats, and down the steps to the sidewalk. Jiggle took my loonie and put a layer of liquid cement glue on the duck side. He then squeezed a few drops onto the sidewalk. He placed the loonie on the drops of cement and stepped on it with one foot. For about ten minutes Jiggle-Me Jason just stood on the loonie in the middle of the sidewalk greeting the people as they walked around him.

"How 'bout this weather, eh?" he said to an elderly lady who passed by and "Working hard or hardly working?" to a police officer.

When the cement had fully dried, Jiggle and I took a seat on the mall steps to watch the show. A few minutes went by before someone noticed the dollar stuck on the sidewalk. The first person was a university-aged woman who looked around real sneaky-like, then bent to pick it up. When she couldn't get it with her hand, she tried to chip it off with her high-heeled shoe. This caused the heel to break off, which made Jiggle and me crack up. The laughing blew our cover. She gave us a ten-second stink-eye, then hobbled to her car, almost slipping on her heelless shoe.

Quite a few people came by and tried to pick up the loonie. It was funny to see how frustrated people get when they can't pick it up—as if it belonged to them. We got cussed out four times in the first hour.

The funniest reaction came from an older gentleman who spied the loonie, then quickened his shuffle to see if it really *was* his lucky day. Once he got to it, he looked around to make sure that it wasn't anybody else's money, and then hit it with his cane. When it didn't move he unscrewed the bottom of his cane and revealed that it also functioned as a pincher. It had two curved plastic arms that pinched together when he squeezed the handle. The pincher thing struck Jiggle as comical, and he started to snicker. The old guy looked up at us and immediately understood the situation.

"You punks don't respect nothing, do ya? In my day we respected every nickel we got, we didn't stick 'em to the sidewalk as bait to go fishing for our elders!" he said.

"Sorry, sir," I yelled as Jiggle and I ran back up the stairs and into the mall. I felt a little bit bad because the old guy thought we were trying to "catch" the elderly like you would a wide-mouth bass, but nobody got hurt, so I didn't worry about it too much.

Seth was still in front of the shoe shop, pacing like a soon-to-be father waiting to see if his baby was going to make it. We walked in and out of sporting goods stores, Jiggle and I, for the good part of an hour. We didn't speak much as we browsed, we didn't have to. We were at the point of friendship when long silences don't seem that long or silent. It's nice to have a buddy as close as Jiggle; it's like no matter what happens to you in life one thing stays the same.

We have been best friends since Grade 2. We met in the principal's office when I had just moved here. Jiggle got sent down to the office because he had stuck a piece of gum in the spout of the drinking fountain during recess. He left just a tiny opening between the gum and the spout, which created pressure enough to cause a thin stream of cold water to shoot about eight feet high. The other kids thought it was great fun until our teacher got shot right in the eye and lost her contact lens. Jiggle yelled out, "Bull's eye!" when it happened and was consequently sent to the office.

I was sitting wide-eyed in the office, a little scared about my new school. After Jiggle got his standard talking to, the principal asked him to show me back to our class. We had desks beside each other that year, and we have been beside each other ever since. But he wasn't "Jiggle-Me Jason" back then, just Jason Parker.

There were a few factors that contributed to Jason's nickname. The obvious one was Jason's weight. He was not like sumo-wrestler fat; he was more like Babe Ruth fat. Just a bit on the chubby side. Another factor was the "Tickle Me Elmo" craze that had mums punching out other mums for the last Elmo at Toys R Us before Christmas. But the real reason Jason Parker was dubbed Jiggle-Me Jason came from our first gym class in junior high.

The teachers were all tiptoeing around the sex education issues during that time, telling us that we might start seeing some changes happen soon—hair in our pits, deeper voices; that we would start noticing girls, and all that kind of crap—like I didn't know everything about sex-ed from Frazier and TV. Anyway, because we were growing up, they said we needed to put on deodorant and change out of our normal clothes before gym. Not like in elementary when you could play soccer for an hour at lunch in your jeans, and then sit your sweaty butt down at your desk. So our first day of gym we all went to the boys' change room to get changed into our gym clothes, but Jason forgot a change of under-wear, or as we call it, "gonch." He still wanted to go to class because we were playing touch football, so he made the decision to "go commando" and just wear his gym shorts. As many can attest, gym shorts without gonch do not provide support where a guy wants the maximum support. While he was jogging around the field in his wobbly situation, Jason kept singing, "Jiggle balls, jiggle balls, jiggle all the way" to the tune of "Jingle Bells." It was pretty gross, but since we were in Grade 7 we thought it was hilarious. From that day on everyone has called him "Jiggle-Me Jason." Even some of the teachers, mostly the ones who try to be hip with the kids, call him by that name.

THE BRAND on Seth's glove looked pretty nice. Seth was beaming like a toddler with an ice cream cone when we met him.

"This is the freakin' sweetest thing ever!" he said.

"Yeah, it looks pretty good," I agreed.

"It looks like you spilled chocolate milk on that thing," Jiggle-Me said just to mess with him.

"Shut up, Jiggle, you know it looks sweet. It looks sweet, right, Brook?"

"I told ya, it looks great. Now can we get out of here?" I replied.

"I can get you guys a deal if you want the same thing done on your gloves, I'm pretty tight with the manager," Seth said, thinking he *really* was tight with the manager.

"And I can get you a deal with your mum, Seth; I'm pretty tight with her too," Jiggle snapped back, and we both bust a gut laughing, pushing and leaning on each other all the way back to the truck.

Seth just said, "Freak off, ya freakin' morons."

Before we dropped Seth off, Jiggle said he was sorry for the joke about his mum, but the set-up was too perfect. Seth accepted the apology and got out of the truck. We headed to the ball diamond.

I needed to begin the first week of my season-long commitment of mowing and raking the field because of the shaving cream prank. Our first regular-season game was in three days so the diamond had to be ready. In my pocket were the keys to the equipment shed that had all the groundskeeping gear stored under the bleachers. The padlock was ultra-heavy-duty because kids always try to break in to steal stuff or just smoke pot. I went in first because Jiggle was scared of mice. It smelled like gasoline and grass from the ride-on lawn mower, and maybe a little bit of mouse poop. I pointed to the ground and yelled, "Mouse," and Jiggle screamed like a girl and ran out of the shed.

"Don't be such a pansy," I said.

"Don't play with me like that," he replied. "You know I hate mice. It's like a phobia or something. I inherited it from my ancestors."

"Whatever. You want to mow or rake?"

"Mow."

"Fine. I'll rake."

Jiggle saluted me as he drove by on the mower. He had a long weed stuck between his teeth and he crossed his eyes, pretending to be one of those dim-witted farmers from the sitcoms. He was skilled at mowing; he never slowed down on the corners and didn't miss a blade of grass in the whole park. The mower was adjustable, and Jiggle kept the blade high so the long grass would slow down any balls in the outfield. He wanted to minimize the extra base hits. I grabbed a fine-tooth rake and a drag rake. You don't actually have to rake the whole infield like you would rake leaves. The drag rake is a big square piece of chicken wire that you just drag behind you as you walk around the base paths. That part I did as fast as I could. Next, I walked to my favourite part in the diamond. To my stage, to my pedestal, to the mound.

I remember the first time I was asked to pitch in Little League. I was more gangly at ten than I am now, and I spent most of my

Little League career on the bench, except for the two innings in right field each game that, because of league regulations, I was guaranteed to play. The game was almost over and all of the pitchers on the team had pitched, so Coach asked me if I wanted to give it a try. I was more nervous than I had ever been and my heart was pounding in my throat. I just went to the mound, closed my eyes, and fired. The first pitch was a perfect strike, and when it snapped into the mitt, the catcher made a little squeal of pain. My coach started to cough in the dugout, as if he had choked on his surprise. I struck out all three batters and nobody even got as much as a foul tick off me. Kids started to fear standing in the batter's box because they didn't want to get hit with my pitches. The coach of the all-star team asked me to play for him in the summer, and I developed the reputation of the hardest-throwing kid my age in Lethbridge. The only thing good about my lanky body is that my gangly arm functions like a whip to generate incredible velocity. Now, I can throw my fastball in the low eighties. My best was eighty-three miles per hour at the fair last year.

The dirt on the mound was different from the dirt in the infield. It was finer, softer. I used the fine-tooth rake to smooth out each bump, pushing and packing the dirt until it was a perfect rounded oval. It took me a while, but I didn't care. I needed to pamper it. It was like a painter's canvas to me. It's only a ten-inch pile of soil, but when I step on it, my whole world is elevated much more than ten inches. I was just the skinny kid who hung out with the funny fat kid before I found my fastball and the mound. Now I wasn't the most popular kid at school, but at least I had something. Something that is more than just part of me, but *is* me. When I stand on the rubber ten inches above the batter, I'm "the man" for once in my life, at least for seven innings. People know me and respect me when I throw a white and red ball sixty feet six inches to a kid in a mask. I might even get to go to college because of the things I do on the mound. That's why I took my time. That's why it had to be perfect.

That was why I ignored Jiggle-Me when he yelled, "Brook, you finished making love to that rake?"

Five

TOOLS OF IGNORANCE—The catcher's paraphernalia: shinguards, chest protector, helmet, mask and glove.

Our school has had a tradition since 1920 of putting the picture of any sports team that places in the top three at Provincials up on the wall in the main hallway. It is called the "Wall of Champions." People spend hours looking at the photos, laughing at the tiny tight shorts from the fifties, the teen moustaches from the seventies, and the perms and neon clothes from the eighties. The only baseball team that was pictured on the Wall of Champions was the 1978 Mustangs—with their star player, Coach K., with long sideburns and a scowl on his face.

I ached to be on that wall. And I ached to get back to playing on the team. The weekly routine of raking the infield and the mound was only making the ache worse. It was like making a starving man fry forbidden doughnuts, or tying the hands of a person with a thousand mosquito bites on their feet. I could practise, and that at least temporarily scratched the itch, but I still couldn't play in the games. I had already missed three regular-season games.

School days in April go by much slower because it's baseball season. School is never the most exciting thing for me, but during the season, I spend most of my class time glancing toward the clock in the back of the room, hoping it's time for practice. I had been working hard at practices for the last month, hustling out every fly ball, getting dirty sliding, and diving for any balls hit my way. In batting practice, I was throwing well and I think Coach was impressed. After I froze Oberg with a slider on the hands, Coach said, "Nice location, Brook." At the three games I had missed so far, I was cheering for my teammates, but laying off the instructions. I was keeping the diamond looking like Fenway, and I hoped Coach was getting ready to give me my second chance.

While sitting in English, my least favourite class, I was staring out the window as my teacher droned on about alliteration. Coach K. had promised a surprise at practice today; I was thinking maybe a home run derby from second base, or a scrimmage.

Daydreaming about the surprise made Mr. Hedley's poetry lesson a little easier to swallow. On my handout was a poem by Sappho. It read:

Without warning
as a whirlwind
swoops on an oak
Love shakes my heart

Why can't poets just say "I fell in love" instead of all this "swooping whirlwind" garbage? Poetry has never made sense to me, it's like, why perform a ballet routine before throwing the fastball when it works just as well if you just aim and fire?

"Mr. Gunderson, are you with us this afternoon?" Mr. Hedley asked, startling me awake from my daydream.

"Yes sir, I am, sir." I say "sir" a lot when I think I'm in trouble.

"Then you wouldn't mind enlightening the class on your opinion as to why Sappho uses the word 'whirlwind' in the second line?"

"Well . . . um . . . in my personal opinion, I believe that, and this is just my opinion, that whirlwinds, by their nature are more swooping animals . . . er, not animals, but wind-things. They are more 'swoopish' than other words that the author could have used," I answered. I could feel my ears turning red.

The whole class cracked up. I was not sure if they were laughing with me, or at me. Man, that was bad. When I get nervous a million words dart around in my head like a million lasers caught in a room of mirrors. I just grasp at whatever I can, and that's what comes out of my mouth. Most of the time it doesn't work out too well.

"Mr. Gunderson, I suggest you pay more attention in my class in the future. There are things more important than baseball, you know."

I wanted to say, "What, like poetry? How many poets make twelve million a year?" but instead I said, "Yes sir."

FINALLY THE BELL RANG, signalling the end of the school day and the beginning of my day—practice. I hustled out of biology class and stopped at my locker to grab my spikes and glove. To start the practice, we all stood in a circle to do stretches. I pulled my right arm over my chest with my left, then swung my arms in full circles forward and backwards. After stretching, we jogged from one foul pole to the other five times, and then we played catch. I partnered with Jiggle, who was trying to make me laugh by squeezing his pants between his butt cheeks making a bunched-up wedgie.

He threw the ball to me and then turned around, pointing to his behind. "Hungry bum, Brook. Beware of the hungry bum."

"You are a moron," I said.

"You don't have a sandwich or something, do ya? My butt is famished."

I threw one as hard as I could at his pants-eating rear end and he almost didn't turn around fast enough dodge it.

"Sheesh! I was just trying to help feed the needy, you didn't have to get so testy," Jiggle said in a mock hurt tone.

It was a warm night and most of us were wearing just three-quarter-length T-shirts. Sonya had her usual Cubs T-shirt on, but she had rolled the sleeves up to her shoulders. She had toned arms, not like freaky women's body-builder-type arms, but defined and smooth.

I wonder why girls' skin always seems smoother than ours, I thought, as I threw grounders to Jiggle. Maybe it's the lack of hair.

Suddenly, Coach's whistle pierced the air, and my eardrum.

"Bring it in, guys," he said. "Now I told you I had a surprise for you tonight and I want to explain it. I was reading in the *Baseball News* recently and was interested to find that 60 percent of games are won by two runs or less. So this inspired my theme for the practice: 'Doing the Little Things.'" Coach used his fingers as quotation marks in the air when he told us the title of the practice. "Now, I want you to get into partners. One partner from each group grab a tennis ball out of the bag."

Once we had the tennis balls, we were instructed to get one bat per group and to stand in a pitcher-batter formation. Jiggle-Me started with the ball and I stood five metres away from him with my bat.

"The object of this drill is to knock the flinching instinct out of you. Pitchers, aim at the batter's shoulder and bean him until he ceases to flinch. Then back up five feet."

A few guys groaned. I tried to look as keen as I could; I thought it might be some kind of final test.

At first it was kind of fun, letting the tennis ball hit you in the shoulder over and over again—it didn't even hurt too bad. After about ten minutes of the beaning drill, Coach called Zander to the batting cage.

Thinking he was free from the drill and got to practise hitting, Zander gloated in our general direction, "See ya later, suckaz."

His smile quickly faded when he saw his new drill, designed especially for catchers. Inside the batting cage, Coach had aimed the pitching machine at the dirt in front of the plate. Zander's job as a catcher was to block the pitches with his body, so in a game situation, no one could steal on a wild pitch. He crouched behind the plate with his full gear on, chest protector, mask, and shin pads—the tools of ignorance, as they say. Most importantly, he was wearing his cup, the catcher's American Express card—you never leave home without it. The ball came zipping in at seventy miles per hour and Zander fearlessly threw his body in front of it. The first time was fearless, the next fifty, not so much. The balls were the heavy dimpled yellow kind, the ones used in batting cages, not the normal white with red stitches kind. Zander took a beating for forty-five minutes, until he blocked twenty in a row. Never had a batting cage felt more like its name. It was more than a cage, it was a torture chamber.

"The best way to take a pitch," Coach told the rest of us, "is to turn your shoulder so the ball will hit you on the meaty part, not the bone. That way, worst it can do is leave a bruise." Then we cranked it up a notch—Coach grabbed a hardball.

"However, in a game situation, it's not a fluffy tennis ball coming at you. Who is man enough to stand in front of this?" Coach K. whipped a fastball that clanged against the backstop and made Seth jump. It wasn't a rhetorical question; he really wanted a volunteer.

"You mean you want to throw a very fast pitch at one of us?" Nabbi asked.

Coach just kept pounding the ball in his glove. There must be some kind of law against what K. was planning to do, I thought, but I knew the drill was somehow meant for me.

"I'll do it," I said before I could think about the consequences. I walked to the batter's box and put my helmet on my head. If I was going to be back on the team, this is what I had to do.

The first pitch hurtled from Coach K.'s hand and came directly at my shoulder. I wanted to let it hit me, but my body wouldn't let it. I jumped out of the way at the last second, and the ball whizzed by me.

"What the heck was that, Brook? Stand in there," Coach hollered. A few of the guys snickered. The next pitch I almost stood in there, but I flinched and the ball went past.

"All right, Brook, get outta there, give someone else a chance," Coach said.

"No! I got this, give me one more chance," I pleaded.

He gave me five more chances—and the first four I dodged. On the fifth, I concentrated hard. I decided just to close my eyes, that way my body wouldn't know when to jump out of the way. With my eyes shut tight, I heard Coach say, "Last chance, Gunderson," and I knew he wasn't only talking about the drill. My ears picked up the scuff of his cleats on the rubber as he started his windup, and I found out it was much scarier in the dark. When I heard him grunt, I knew the ball was on the way, and I panicked. I hit the dirt, getting a mouthful of the plate, and the ball sailed safely over my head. I couldn't do it . . . I had failed.

The rest of the practice went by in a blur. I started to think that I should just quit and play for a coach who wasn't such a tyrant. At the end of practice, Coach gave us a pep talk about the next four games, which, according to him, were only preparation for the big one—the game against the Northside Bulldogs. He tried to inspire us with phrases like "Baseball games are won with strong hearts, not skilled hands" and "We are only as strong as our weakest link." I could hardly stand to listen to Coach vomit out clichés, I just wanted to get home and lie down.

The sun was going down on the field, and on my baseball season, as Coach K. moseyed over to me on the bleachers. He was flipping a brand-new Rawlings in his hand like a quarter.

"You volunteered to try the drill today, when nobody else would. That took some *cojones*," he said in a flat tone.

"I'm sorry, Coach, I wanted to, but my body wouldn't let me do it," I said, my voice wavering a bit.

"This is Tuesday's game ball," he said, putting it into my hand. "Take this home and see if you can convince it to cross the plate for you. . . . You deserve it."

A huge smile broke across my face until I could feel it stretch my ears. "You mean I can pitch?"

"I mean you are *allowed* to pitch, you'll have to prove that you *can* pitch on Tuesday."

I actually skipped from the end of my driveway to our front door like Dorothy and the Tin-Man skipped down the yellow brick road in my mum's theatre production of *The Wizard of Oz*. That was how happy I was. If I knew how to do a heel-click I probably would have, but it's a pretty sissy thing to do and Frazier was sitting in the front window reading Orwell's *Animal Farm*.

"What's with the overly blissful state, little man?" Frazier asked, as I bounced into the front hall.

"Coach K. just let me know I'm allowed to pitch again," I said, not even trying to hide my excitement from my big bro.

"What do you mean he 'allowed' you to pitch again? That sounds to me like a case of the ruling class deciding what we underlings can and can't do." Frazier was really getting into his book, I guess.

"Naw, it's nothing like that. I just made some mistakes at the beginning of the year, but I made up for it and I'll be back on the mound. No biggy. What's up with you? How you liking the ranching business?" I asked, even though I knew he wasn't a big fan of his new job because of his foreman, Tiny Pete.

Frazier had recently started working for a large ranch outside of town, mostly moving irrigation pipe from pasture to pasture and cleaning up around the place. The worst part for him was the fact that Tiny Pete never left his little office or took off his perfect little cowboy boots and hat to do any of the hard work that Frazier and the crew had to do. Frazier would always say he felt like part of the modern-day proletariat, whatever that means.

"Job is okay, I guess. But let me ask you something. We had an incident at work today and I'd like to get your opinion on something. Does a person have the right to laugh at something he or she finds humorous?" he said.

"Sure," I replied, getting ready for one of Frazier's famous logical arguments where he leads you from point to point so you have to agree with him.

"What if a person finds it humorous when another person unwittingly zaps himself on an electric fence? Is it permissible to laugh then?"

"As long as the fence didn't really injure him. I think it would be fair to laugh at the situation," I replied.

"Now what if the person who was zapped was your foreman, Tiny Pete? Additionally, what if as Tiny Pete was coming out to the field to scold you for some indiscretion, he tried to straddle the electric fence and, due to the shortness of his legs, he found his crotch to be at a perfect height to conduct the current? Would a person be in the wrong if he guffawed at the sight of his foreman straddling an electric fence, bug-eyed with electricity flowing through his nether regions?" Frazier said in a tone that reminded me of a lawyer on TV. Fraze is totally deadpan when it comes to his sense of humour.

"What the frick are you talking about!? You mean he fried his unit?" I laughed out loud at the thought of it.

"Actually, he was zapped four times before he got off the fence. You see, he didn't know that they had put a new electric fence in that field, and when he first felt the electricity flow through his groin, all two thousand volts of it, as he stepped over the wire, his natural reaction was to jump up, away from the zap. The jump gave him temporary relief from the pain, but then he would come down again for another round. His eyes would bug out even more and his screams became even higher pitched with each unfortunate landing. He jumped three times, zizzt, zizzt, zizzt, before he figured out it would be wiser to dive onto the ground and save his poor, barbecued manhood."

I was rolling on the floor as he told me the story so matter-of-factly. Some of the boys and I had once held hands in a chain and then grabbed an electric fence on a dare, and it stings pretty bad. "I can't believe he kept jumping up and landing on it," I said through snorts of laughter.

"So you can understand why a person would be justified in laughing a little at the scene then?" Frazier said, not really needing an answer. "I wish my boss could see my perspective. Instead, he forced me to shovel cow manure out of the barns for the rest of the day. But other than that, work's fine."

He finally let a small smirk escape from his face when he finished the story. He stood up from the chair he was reading in and said, "I made some tacos if you're hungry. They're in the kitchen."

I thought I could smell the faint odour of sweet smoke when he walked by me into the kitchen. It was the smell you smell if you go to the beach in Vancouver, or go to the Alberta Folk Festival, but it was mixed with a taco seasoning smell and the Glade Plug-in "Spring Flowers" that was plugged into the outlet beside Frazier's chair. The fan was on full blast and all the windows were wide open. I thought, I bet he thinks I don't know what's going on. My mum had a show that night, Taylor was at piano lessons and my dad was working late, so Frazier figured he could smoke a doobie in the house and nobody would know. I didn't really care what he smoked, I just didn't like that he thought I was too stupid to figure it out.

We both sat down on the bar stools at the kitchen counter. Frazier had some ice cream because he had already eaten his supper while I downed a soft taco. It was already seven at night and I was starving. Fraze was holding his book in one hand and his spoon in the other. He wasn't looking at the bowl because he was concentrating on his reading, so he often missed the ice cream and sometimes he scooped a spoonful of air into his mouth.

"Dad would flip if he knew you lit up in the house," I blurted out. I had never talked about drugs with Frazier in my life. It was one of the topics that I usually tiptoed around, always thinking it, but never saying it. Like when someone you know has cancer but when you're around him or her you just pretend that nothing is wrong, that it is forbidden to mention the illness.

"What are you talking about, pal?" Frazier said, acting surprised. "I'm clean. Been clean for months now."

"Look, I don't care if you smoke weed, I'm just saying Dad will have kittens if he finds out," I said, trying to sound totally cool with it. I didn't want him to think I would rat him out or something.

"Did you know our physician father could prescribe marijuana? You know, to heal the sick. Now I'm not saying that I do or don't use, but if I wasn't feeling too hot, which is often the case, why would it be a problem to use a little medicinal cannabis? Indigenous peoples have used it for thousands of years in their cultures, but in our culture some government official deemed it immoral and now it is evil. The same government that rakes in millions on the taxes they charge on alcohol and nicotine, both drugs that are much more dangerous and much more *legal* than marijuana." Fraze was using the professor voice he has. I always feel stupid when he uses that voice on me.

"Dude, I was just saying that Dad and Mum will kill you if they catch you. You don't have to get all preachy on me." I kind of laughed after I said "preachy." It seemed a bit ironic that in this town someone was on their soapbox preaching in favour of dope instead of against it. I bet Frazier is the only one in this city who would preach the good word of weed.

"Just wanted you to have an open mind, little buddy." I hate when he calls me little buddy. He still thinks I'm a kid.

He went back to reading his book and I finished my taco then, after putting away both of our dishes (Frazier never puts his dishes in the dishwasher), I went down to my room gripping the game ball Coach K. gave me across the four seams. Lying with my head on the pillow, I tossed the ball straight up in the air, and as I tried to skim the ceiling with the laces, I made a plan. I needed to keep my nose clean no matter what. Baseball was much more important than a few fizzy Pop Rocks in my belly. Baseball could be my one-way ticket to college. I wouldn't give Kobrinsky any reason to even frown in my direction. If that meant staying home when Jiggle had an idea for a prank, then I'd have to stay home.

Six

THROWING GAS—A pitcher who is throwing fast; also known as throwing smoke or throwing aspirin. When a pitcher throws so hard the ball becomes hard to see, like an aspirin from the mound.

Game day. My opening day. A small dose of Pop Rocks exploded in my stomach all day as I walked around school. Faces passed by in waves. People I knew by name, but had never spoken to, lined the hallways talking about movies and the latest gossip. Girls stood in packs giggling about boys, and boys said outrageous things loud enough so the girls could hear while pretending that they didn't notice the girls. Only one thing occupied my thoughts.

Not even 5 percent of the student body knew we were playing the Running Rebels from a small town outside of ours at five that day. We'd have twenty people in the stands tonight if we were lucky, I thought. Like I said, the hockey players are the heroes around here. But that didn't matter. I'd be the starting pitcher tonight, working my fastballs in and out, making the hitter guess.

I always passed Sonya in the main hallway before fourth period. She was usually with Nabbi because they both had wood shop together. I never saw her with girls, she was a "one of the guys" type; all her close friends were on the team.

She was holding a wooden piggy bank shaped like a duck that she had cut out on the scroll saw. "Brook, what's up?" she said.

"Nothing much," I replied. "Nice duck."

"Thanks. You stoked for tonight?" she asked.

"I'm pretty nervous," I admitted. "Do you need a ride? We could swing by if you want."

As soon as I said the last sentence, a Grade 12 girl in a tight sweater and matching pink skirt, with matching friends, called out, "You're barking up the wrong tree, dweeb, that one's a dyke." Everyone around got a good laugh at that.

It ticked me off big time so I turned to them and said, "I'm sorry, I didn't catch what you said because I was trying to comprehend how a person with a brain that small could have a butt that ginormous." I didn't care if they were popular and their boyfriends would probably beat me senseless later, I hate it when people act like that.

The leader of the Barbies said, "What-*ever*," drawing out the word. She acted like the "ginormous" comment didn't faze her but I saw her steal a glance at her backside as they walked to their SUV.

"They're just scared that I'm going to try and get with them." Sonya shrugged as if it was no big deal. "Yeah, I could use a ride to the game tonight, see ya around four?"

"Sure," I said, kind of in a daze.

So I guess that settled it. Sonya liked girls. It was fine with me; Sonya was still one of the coolest people I knew no matter what. Why should I care if she thought chicks were attractive as long as she kept robbing people of extra base hits? I mean, Sonya could like girls if she wanted. It's the twenty-first century. This didn't change our relationship. Not that we really had one. "Nice duck" was about the only thing I had said to her that didn't relate to baseball in three years of knowing her.

I spent a good half-hour having an inner dialogue about why I didn't care that Sonya was into girls. I don't know why it took a whole half-hour, I don't even think about baseball for that long without a break.

No one was at the diamond when we pulled up. The fence was locked so I climbed over the lowest part, being careful not to rip my pants as I went over. I opened the gate for Jiggle and Sonya and we all walked toward our dugout, our bags hung over our shoulders. Our bats and gloves were in our hands and dust was kicking up behind. I pictured it like a scene from a movie, you know, after a group of tough guys decide they will save the world even though they will probably die in the process; they walk out squinting into the sun, slow-motion steps in synch, maybe one of them spits, while the bass booms on the background track. I'm a bizarre dude sometimes.

When the rest of the team got to the park, we were playing three-way catch in the outfield to get warm. I was on one side and Jiggle and Sonya were down at the other end by the first-base line fence. I threw to one, then the other, giving me two throws for each of their one. We stretched it out a bit with long toss for a while. My arm felt strong, no kinks as I circled it directly above my shoulder, keeping my elbow almost straight, and letting it sail forty metres to Jiggle. My mind drifted to my game plan. Their fourth hitter was the only one who was a threat. He liked to open up his stance to pull the inside fastball. Keep it low and away, work in lots of off-speed stuff, I repeated to myself. If I could control my pitches I should be able to go the distance, the whole seven innings.

I ADJUSTED THE BRIM on my hat as I walked to the mound. I like it pulled down low and curved tight around my eyes. The tunnel vision it creates helps me focus on the strike zone. I mentally went through my plan again; work the pitches low and away from the batters and stick with my best pitch—the four-seam fastball. I love to bring the heat; I do have a slider and a change-up but whenever I'm in trouble I just reach back and gun the fastball.

I pulled the brim of my hat down and curved it around my eyes again with my right hand; my glove was behind my back holding the new white ball. My goal was to keep the grass stains off it. Give it back to the ump after the game looking exactly as it was now.

He pointed at me and called out, "Let's play ball!"

The first pitch of the day, of my high school career, was the four-seamed fastball. It snapped as it hit Zander's catcher's mitt and the umpire grunted something that sounded like "Sthaaw," which for this particular guy meant "Strike." All umpires have their own style, the way they call a person safe or out, the way they signal strike three. If you strike somebody out when this guy was umpiring, he would grab an imaginary cord that came out of his chest and violently pull on it, like you would if you were starting a lawn mower. I loved it.

Zander put one finger down and tapped his right knee, signalling for an outside fastball. The batter tried to drag-bunt it, but missed altogether. Two strikes and no balls. "Time to start the mower," I thought as I dug two fingers on the outside stitches of the ball, preparing for the deuce. The slider fooled the guy and he watched it for strike three, pounding his bat on the plate before he ran into the dugout.

"Attababy, Gunner," an outfielder yelled while the infield threw the ball around the horn.

My nickname when I pitch is "Gunner." Not very imaginative when you consider my last name is Gunderson and I throw hard, but at least it's cooler than Brook.

The next two batters went down the same way, both strikeouts. It was a nice way to start a season. The league record was fifteen strikeouts in a game, which was set four years ago by a guy who is in the Dodgers farm system now. The way I was feeling today, I could break it. I bet my fastball was up around eighty-two miles per hour. I made a mental note to have it clocked again at the summer fair.

Our first three batters got a hit, including Nabbi's double, which scored two runs. Oberg hit a high fly ball that went over the fence but was about two feet foul. Man, that kid had power. We played in a diamond that was 300 feet at the corners and 380 to centre, almost as big as the majors, and Oberg hit ten homers in fifteen games last season. A few scouts are already sniffing around and he's only in Grade 10.

The next pitch he hit a mile high but not out of the infield. The second baseman almost missed it, but at the last second leaned back and caught it behind his head.

With one out, Jiggle slapped a ground ball up the middle, and Seth got on base because the third baseman bobbled his grounder. Next up was Randall, who played third base when I pitched. He struck out watching a fastball that caught the outside corner. He thought it was a ball, and slammed his helmet on the ground beside me as I was warming up in the on-deck circle.

"Take 'er easy pal," I said to him as I made my way to the batter's box. "You'll get him next time." Randall is wound up tighter than a Rawlings official baseball. He's always worrying about what his dad will say after the game. His dad is one of these old almost-pros who want their kids to make up for the failures they had in life. It's pretty tough on Randall, it seems like he doesn't really even like the game much anymore. He just plays because his old man is always on his back.

I stepped up to the plate with Jiggle on third and Seth on first. I looked down at Coach K. on the third-base line for the signals. He did about ten meaningless signs, ear tugs, hat touches, leg wipes, and stuff like that. I was waiting for the indicator; the sign that means the next signal he gives is the real sign. When Coach slid his right arm across the letters on his chest, I knew to be ready for the real sign. He tugged his left ear twice—the steal was on. It was a good strategy because if the catcher tried to throw down to second to catch Seth, then Jiggle on third had a good chance of stealing home. If he didn't throw, then we would have two runners in scoring position. I let the first pitch go by, it was a strike, and Seth took the opportunity to steal second. It didn't draw a throw; the catcher didn't want to risk it. The next pitch he threw was another fastball; I took a swing and fouled it off. Now I had two strikes on me and no balls. I've never been a great hitter. I'm a contact hitter, I rarely strike out, but I don't rip line drives through the infield very often either. My best skill as a hitter comes from being a pitcher. I think like a pitcher and often guess what is coming next.

In this situation, I knew that he was thinking, "Two strikes and no balls. Make him chase something out of the strike zone or use a trick pitch."

He went with his best trick pitch, the sinker. I knew it was coming and took a solid swing at it. I hit it hard toward the shortstop; he picked it up with no trouble, pounded it into his glove a couple times and then let it fly toward first base. I was sprinting down the line, digging in the shale with my spikes. The throw was a few feet high and to the right of the first baseman and he had to take his foot off the bag to catch the ball. The dust flew out of the bag as I stepped on it and continued running into foul territory. Safe! Jiggle trotted in from third to score. I called, "Time" and asked someone in the dugout to bring me my jacket. I wanted to keep my arm warm while I was on the base paths.

Charlton, our lead-off hitter, batted for the second time this inning and hit a double that scored Seth and me. Sonya then grounded out to the first baseman and that ended the inning. Score was Mustangs 5, Rebels 0.

The next five innings went much the same way. All the time off, and the desire Coach instilled in me to pitch well, had made me an animal on the mound. I had fourteen strikeouts so far—one away from tying the record, two from breaking it.

"We're dominating these guys," I said to Zander while we rallied for another four runs in the sixth inning.

"Yeah man, the baseball gods are smiling on us today," he said, totally serious.

"Why do you figure that is, Zander?" I asked.

"You're gonna think I'm a psycho if I tell you."

"No, I won't, just tell me."

"I stuck a Babe Ruth baseball card on my chest with pine tar last night and slept with it."

"Okay, I lied. I do think you're a psycho," I said. "Didn't it stink?"

"Not too bad, but when I pulled it off this morning the five hairs I had on my chest got ripped off with the pine tar."

"Bummer."

"I know! I was hoping for a patch in time for swimsuit season."

"Swimsuit season? Okay, now you're really starting to freak me out," I said and then gave him a moderately hard backhand to the cup, just to scare him. He flinched and knocked his head against the dugout wall.

We were leading 11 to 2 going into the last inning. Coach K. said I should rest the last inning because we were up by so much. I told him about the league strikeout record and practically begged him to let me stay in. He looked at me long and hard through his Coke-bottle glasses and finally said it was okay, but if I injured my pitching arm, he was going to break the other one. I actually believed it.

Everybody had been playing well; the two runs they got came from one fielding error when Seth could have easily caught a ball hit out to right field, but he had his glove off when it came. He was polishing the SOUTHPAW inscription on his glove like people polish their glasses, opening his mouth real wide, then breathing moist breath on it, followed by a jersey scrub to shine it up. Coach K. gave him ten extra wind-sprints on the spot. What a knucklehead. The other run came after I walked their second hitter. The cleanup guy came up, the one who likes to pull the inside pitches, and cranked an inside pitch off the wall in left field. I tried to keep the ball low and away, like I had practised, but even on good days pitchers make mistakes. At least mine only cost me one run.

I stepped on to the mound for the last three outs of the ball game. If they didn't catch up, we wouldn't bat in the last inning. I didn't want to think about the strikeout record but I couldn't help it. Only two strikeouts to beat the record, just six pitches. I was about to face their second, third, and unfortunately their fourth hitters. But if I struck out the first two, I wouldn't have to worry about the big guy.

I stared at the player at the plate, took my hat off, and wiped my forehead. There wasn't actually any sweat because it was April and we were in Alberta. I just wiped because that was what a pro pitcher would do at a time like this. The player stepped in the box and took a few slow practice swings, staring at the ball in my hand. Zander gave me the sign for the slider; I nodded and shifted the ball behind my back until I felt the right grip. When I let go I snapped my wrist as hard as I could, and it spun fast in a counter-clockwise direction bending away from the right-handed batter. Strike one. Some of the tension in my stomach dissolved, I was ahead on him now, in the driver's seat. The slider helped set up my next pitch, the inside fastball. He'd probably think the ball would bend to the middle of the plate like the last one, but it would blow by him while he waited for it to curve. I pitched the inside fastball and he watched it for strike two. I knew I had him now; he was primed to chase something out of the zone. I gave him the "high heat," up around his shoulders; he swung but didn't have a chance, and the ump started the mower for the fifteenth time.

It turned out I did have to face the big guy. The next batter went down, but not on strikes; I wanted to fool him with a change-up on the first pitch but he hit it deep and hard. Charlton made a beauty of a catch in right centre, sliding on his knees as he got there. If it had been any other player it would have dropped in, but Charlton's blazing speed got him there on time.

With none on, two out, two sweaty armpits, and one strikeout to go, I prepared to face their best hitter. Zander called time to talk it over with me.

"Okay pal, this guy eats up anything inside. Keep it low and away," he said.

"Yup, gotcha," my mouth said, but my brain was somewhere else.

"Do you want some Big League Chew?"

"What! From your mouth?"

"Yeah man, I'm telling you it's lucky," he pressured.

I was willing to do anything for the record so I said, "Okay, but don't let anyone see."

He reached under his mask and ripped off a piece of his gum. Then he took the ball, stuck the gum on it, and put the gum-ball in my glove. "You got this," he said.

I know it was gross but I wasn't thinking rationally. I slipped the gum in when I pretended to cough. It was hard and tasted like a mix of leather and Zander—"Zleather." I dry-heaved.

The Running Rebels' fourth hitter had a tattoo on his forearm that bulged each time he took a swing; it looked like it was the Tasmanian Devil or something. Man, is he going to regret that decision when it's just a wrinkled brown blob on his eighty-year-old arm and he has to explain to his grandkids that it's a cartoon character that Granddad thought was cool when he was in high school. Maybe he would just tell them it was a birthmark to save himself some embarrassment.

The first three pitches I threw missed the outside corner by an inch. I thought about just walking him and pitching to a weaker batter for the record, but I didn't want to be a pansy. I'm sure his coach was telling him to let the 3 and 0 pitch go by, so I sent one right down the pipe. I was wrong. He hit it deep and high into right field; it looked like it might go over the fence. Seth ran to get under it and while straddling the chalk of the foul line he jumped, reaching for the ball. It hit his glove and sort of bounced over the fence. Everyone stopped and looked at the umpires. Nobody knew what to do so the tattoo guy started to trot around the bases like he hit a home run. The umps called a meeting at second base and decided that because Seth was in foul territory when he knocked the ball over the fence, it was a foul ball!

"Just a long strike, Brook," Coach called out to the mound.

"Maybe this gum *is* lucky," I thought to myself. I had shown him all fastballs so far, so I decided to go with the slider. It fooled him enough that he didn't swing and it was called for a strike. Full count. The record was on the line. Zander signalled for the slider. He hadn't hit my slider very well tonight. I nodded my head. I sucked in a deep breath and started my windup, slow, methodical. Midway though my windup—going slider all the way—I saw it. He choked up on the bat to shorten his swing; he thought it was a fastball! In the split second before I let the pitch go, I changed my mind—to the change-up. I whipped my arm like I was throwing the hardest pitch I could ever throw but I let my wrist go like a rag doll at the last possible moment, and the ball spun off of my palm. I aimed for his most tempting spot—inside and belt high. When he saw it coming his eyes got wide like my grandma's at bingo; it was his favourite pitch. He took a monster swing expecting to crush it, but caught nothing but a mix of oxygen and carbon dioxide. He swung so far ahead of the pitch that he probably could have swung twice.

Seven

DANDY—A player who values his appearance on the diamond more than his play. A dandy will rarely slide or do anything that might dirty his uniform.

The next morning I woke up and rushed downstairs to get the newspaper. They often printed small articles about our games in the local sports section. My dad already had the paper and was reading about mad cow disease.

"It's pretty sad that thousands of ranchers are going bankrupt when the likelihood of dying from mad cow disease is less than the likelihood of drowning in your toilet, eh pal?" he said to me, peering over the paper. "Why don't they ban toilet swimming instead of beef?" My old man got a jolt from his own joke, chuckling harder than was probably within acceptable limits.

"Was there an article about the game in there, Dad?" I asked.

"Nothing in here, sorry," he said, the cover story hiding his face.

"Really? What the heck?" I said.

"I don't know. Hey, could you get me the milk out of the fridge?"

When I went to the fridge, there, pasted at eye level, was an article with a photo of me in my windup. Dad had already highlighted all the parts about me in bright yellow.

"Great game last night, pal. Can you sign my paper before I go to the hospital? I want to put it on eBay to pay for a new yacht," he said, holding out the entertainment section.

"Don't be a goof," I said, trying to hold back my smile.

My dad is an oncologist at the hospital, which means he works with cancer patients every day. You'd think it would get him down, but he is always cheerful. Except for when you knot twenty of his neckties into a rope and use them to pull your friends behind your bike on a skateboard. He gets pretty steamed if you do that.

The article in the paper read:

West High Mustang Brook Gunderson struck out 16 to set a new Alberta league record in an 11 to 2 victory over the Running Rebels. The record was set four years ago by Kale Marshal who is now with the Columbus Catfish of the L.A. Dodgers' farm system. Gunderson started out the game with three straight K's setting the tone for the rest of the game. The Mustangs' offence was almost as sharp as the right-handed pitcher, inking 5 runs in the first inning and 11 in total. Much of that offence was contributed by the Mustangs' Nabbi Ghedi and Shane Oberg who went 4 for 5 and 3 for 4 respectively, at the plate last night. Local fans are anxiously awaiting the matchup between the West High Mustangs and the Northside Bulldogs on May 12. Both teams are considered to have a shot at winning this year's Provincial Championship.

That was the first time I had more than just my name in the paper, and I've got to admit that I was really stoked about it. I put it back on the fridge, right in the middle, covering up Mum's grocery list. I wondered if the people at school had read it. Maybe next time I'd get an interview.

"A world record holder right here in my house! This is pretty neat-oh." It was my mother walking in from the den. She doesn't really "get" high school baseball, or the world record system in general.

She was wearing one of those hands-free telephones so she could talk while she helped Taylor with her math homework. Homework that should have been done last night, but because Taylor plays the piano, has singing lessons, and is in her school play right now, the part about being home for homework never seems to work out, except in the morning. I sometimes feel bad for the little thing. She's like the golden child in our house. My parents have long given up on Frazier becoming anything, and ever since I can remember, the only A I have received on a report card was in gym. Taylor gets straight As and is very musically talented so most of the parenting resources are funnelled into her. Sometimes I think it wears her out, holding the weighty Gunderson family ambitions on her shoulders all by herself.

"Brook, are you gonna be in the *Guinness Book of Records*?" Taylor asked, following right on Mum's heels.

"No, you guys, it's not a world record, it's just an Alberta high school baseball record. It's no big deal," I said. I try to be modest in the face of so much adoration.

"That's a big deal in my books. Alberta is a big place and—" Mum was cut off mid-sentence by the patio door squeaking open to the kitchen, where everybody was standing.

It was Frazier, wearing the same clothing he'd gone out in the night before, trying to sneak into the house. Usually the kitchen patio door was the best bet to get past my parents' bedroom and had the most direct route to the basement, but not today. We all knew that Frazier's job started at 6:00 a.m. and the clock above the fridge read 7:43. My gut started to feel heavy because I knew what this meant—he had lost his job, again. Fraze poked his head through the door and saw all four of us staring back at him.

"Oh, hello family," he said, in a higher pitch than normal. His eyes looked weird. Almost like the ring of blue in his eyes that usually dazzles the ladies was swallowed up by the pupils. His nose was red and running, but he was smiling. "We having breakfast together, like the old days?"

Everybody was silent. Taylor could sense a blow-up and quickly left and went back to her math assignment in the other room. My dad slowly shifted the paper to the table and took a sip of his orange juice, as if he was contemplating what to say or do.

"Tiny Pete giving you the day off?" I asked hopefully, trying to cut the tension and give Frazier a way out.

"You could say that," Frazier replied, forcing the words to come out slowly, like a jockey pulling back on a racehorse. Then he quickly added, "Man, do I ever have bad hay fever today. Your flowers are really blooming, Mum."

"Son, why aren't you at work this morning?" Dad asked in a not-so-gentle tone. "You *are* aware of the fact that I had to call in more than a few favours to get you that position, aren't you?"

"Yeah, Dad, I know. And I appreciate it and everything, but . . ."

"What do you mean 'but'?" Dad was getting a little riled up. Not skateboarding-with-his-knotted-up-neckties riled, more like Brook-just-used-the-wood-laid-out-for-a-new-fence-to-light-a-fire-for-mallow-roasting riled. "Why didn't you go into work today?"

"Dad, it is just tough working in that situation. Tiny Pete breaks about a hundred labour laws every day with what he forces us to do, and without coffee breaks. And I wouldn't even care about the hard work if Pete didn't sit on his fanny reading *Modern Mechanic* all day. It's like we are in a caste system in some third-world country and I have no rights, or like we've gone back to Stalin's Russia." Frazier's words gushed out like a sports announcer trying to keep up with the action on the court. He sniffed every two or three words and was constantly brushing his nose with the back of his hand.

It seemed to me that Frazier wasn't really seeing the reality of his work situation and that marijuana was probably not his only choice of substances last night.

"So did you quit or were you fired?" Dad asked.

"A combination, I guess," Frazier answered. "When he started to fire me, I yelled out *'Sic semper tyrannis.'* That's what John Wilkes Booth said before he assassinated Lincoln—it means 'thus always to tyrants.' Then I added 'I quit, my friend, I quit. I will not stand for this blatant workplace inequality for one more second.'" Frazier seemed quite pleased with himself as he waited, shoulders back, for my dad to reply.

Dad took a long pull at his orange juice, like a president might take a swill of scotch before ordering a dangerous, but necessary, air strike. "Son, I am afraid that your mother and I have coddled you for much too long. You seem to have a very skewed vision of the real world and I've decided, after listening to what you've got to say, that it will serve you much better to be given a chance to fend for yourself. In one week's time, the cost of living in this home is five hundred dollars a month. You may stay here if you wish for as long as you want, but you will probably find more affordable lodgings in the community. You have one week to decide." Dad let the words hang in the silence, making the air seem thick and cold. He had always taken care of us no matter what. He paid for everything we needed and most everything we wanted. He'd even paid for Frazier's tuition when he went to college.

The unabashed reality that came from Dad's ultimatum scared me. I looked at Frazier, who was looking straight at Dad—two bull elk trying to intimidate the other with the strength of their glares—and then over to Mum, who was intently staring down at the table linen and thumbing it as if she was contemplating the stitching.

Frazier finally spoke in a low, calm voice just above a whisper, "I won't need a week to decide, Doctor Gunderson. I'll start fending for myself this very instant." He no longer wiped his nose or sniffed, and he seemed as sober as a nun on a Tuesday. "And just so you know, I never asked to be coddled, you made that choice yourself," he added and turned and walked back out the patio door.

That was the last I saw of Frazier for a week. His stuff disappeared from his room, so he must have snuck in to collect his belongings later. From then on, it seemed that his absence caused more tension in our home than his presence ever did.

COACH AND I DECIDED that I would rest my arm the next two games so I could be fresh for the big one in two weeks.

We easily won our first game, 9–3. Randall pitched and I played third base. I also got two hits and drove in one run. Oberg hit his first home run of the regular season in the top of the first, crushing it over the left-field fence. It landed on the street, just missing a garbage truck.

In the second game, we played the worst team in the league, the Tigers. It was a relaxing game for the starters because we only played three innings, and then Coach K. put in all the guys who usually warm the bench. We had a good time in the dugout trying to spit sunflower seeds into a cup and seeing who could put the most gumballs in his mouth. We won 13–4.

As we were finishing packing up our stuff to go, we heard a *thump thump thump*, coming from a car stereo down the street. It was a purple Honda Civic hatchback with a silver racing stripe. I recognized the car immediately. It belonged to our team's common arch enemy, Luke Fabro. A large fin on the back of the car was a new addition this year. The fancy racing fins are technically called spoilers. I guess because the only people who can afford them are utterly spoiled, like Luke. Spoiled in the sense that his divorced parents give him whatever he wants, and spoiled in that his insides are rotten, like an egg left out in the sun.

Luke was the Bulldogs' best player and pitcher. He never struck out, and he almost threw as hard as I did, but he had a better curveball. The problem with him was he didn't care about pitching; it was just another thing he was better at than everyone else. Last year he was offered a contract to play in the Western Hockey League, but his mum said he had to finish high school before he could play professional hockey. So he had one more year to wait, which would allow him some more time to grow his blond locks long enough to poke out the back of his helmet and blow in the wind as he skated.

He also had an additional silver stripe painted on the hood of his car for every new girl he made out with; he pretended the meaning was secret, but he conveniently leaked the info out and now everyone knew what they represented. I counted eight stripes as he parked his car on an angle using two spaces instead of one. What a jerk.

Fabro was flanked by his usual two shadows, Brett and Blake, as they walked up to Jiggle and me. Blake and Brett didn't get anything from their relationship with Luke, except the status of being associated with him and the odd chance to date his leftovers.

"It's Brook, right?" Fabro said to me, pretending he didn't know the name of the guy he had played baseball against since Tee Ball. "Man, that's a weird name for a dude—were your parents hoping for a girl?" Blake and Brett guffawed.

"Real original, Fabro," I said back, trying to sound tough but casual. "I hope you didn't hurt your head composing that opening line on the way over here."

Luke and the boys just continued laughing; they really thought I had never heard that one before.

"What the hell are you doing here anyway?" I asked (I don't usually say "hell" but in these tough-guy situations if you say "heck" you're going to get laughed out of town).

"We just came to tell you the weather forecast for the game on Saturday," Fabro said, smiling like an advertisement of a used-car salesman on the back of a bus. "Looks like there might be a breeze— you should think about putting some rocks in your pocket so you don't blow off the mound." A few fans heard him and snickered while Blake and Brett high-fived.

Man, why did he have to bring up my skinniness? He knew that was where I was most vulnerable. I got so flustered that all I could think to say was "Shut up, maybe you're gonna blow off the mound, turd bait."

"Seriously, you and your fatty friend look like the number ten walking around," he drawled, pointing to Jiggle and me. He tucked his hair behind his ears and, without looking, beeped the automatic lock on his car. "See you fairies on Saturday."

My heart was pounding in my chest as they walked away. There was nothing I would have liked more than to punch that guy out, but considering the twigs I have for arms, I'd settle for a strikeout.

"Where were you when he was calling us a walking number ten?" I said to Jiggle. "I thought you had my back."

"Sorry, buddy, I was picturing the wind blowing you off the mound," he joked. "Besides, I got a plan."

Eight

RHUBARB—A ruckus with the umpire(s) or a fight between players or between the players and fans. Most likely stemming from the stage practice of having extras shout "rhubarb" out of step with one another to create the general atmosphere of a hubbub.

The night before the grudge match between the good guys—the Mustangs of West High—and the bad guys—the Bulldogs of the Northside—I found myself unlocking the familiar equipment shed of our ball diamond with the keys Coach had entrusted to me, and silently pushing the mower into the moonlight. Tonight, however, we wouldn't be mowing and raking our diamond to complete our weekly duty—tonight's job was pure volunteer work, pro bono.

I held tightly to Jiggle's shoulders while we moved down the centre of the broad streets as fast as the ride-on lawn mower would take us. I straddled the machine and stood behind Jiggle on the wheel coverings, while he drove the John Deere. He was wearing a pink bike helmet that belonged to his little sister, and I had on an old football helmet that he'd found underneath the stage in our main gym. It was the kind with just one thick bar in front of your chin that only the kickers wear now. Jiggle said that if the cops caught us, at least we wouldn't get tickets for not wearing head protection.

Thankfully, we made it to the Bulldogs' field without incident, apart from a neighbourhood dog that chased us for a block barking so loudly I was sure someone would wake up and find us out. I jumped off the back of the mower and stood on top of the bleachers as a watchman, while Jiggle did the dirty work. He drove out to far left field and lowered the blades to less than a centimetre. The motor groaned as the blades struggled to cut through the long grass and down to the dirt, spitting up rocks and dust in a whirlwind around Jiggle. The noise was loud and unnatural sounding. I quickly directed my eyes toward the closest houses, about one hundred metres away—no lights yet. Jiggle worked in left field for a few minutes, and when the dust cleared I saw, in dark brown dirt against the background of green grass, a neatly cut letter "N" covering a huge spot in the outfield. Jiggle picked up the blades and moved to far right field. He wanted to make sure that he didn't run out of room to write the entire message in the grass, so he was working his way from the ends to the middle of the message.

Jiggle had told me he was going to write something in the Bulldogs' outfield on the way there, but he didn't tell me what he would write. He wanted it to be a surprise. Four of the five letters were shaved into the grass—so far it spelled "N-_-R-D-S." I was kind of disappointed in Jiggle. I hoped he would think of something better than that to get into the Bulldogs' heads.

THERE WERE TWO reactions to the creative writing in the outfield when the fans started pouring into the ball diamond. Most were disgusted, and some were delighted. Although they frantically tried, there was nothing the groundskeepers could do to hide the work of Jiggle-Me Jason before the game. The Northside centre fielder stood in position between the gigantic "A" and "R" that spelled "NARDS" in the outfield during the warm-up. Why nards? I don't know. But I do think it is a pretty embarrassing word to have carved in your outfield, and it was much better than "nerds," which was what I thought it was going to be.

This was Lethbridge high school baseball fans' most anticipated game of the regular season, which meant they came in droves— well, droves of two and three—filling most of the centre of the grandstand for a total of about eighty people. I guess most people were at home watching hockey reruns or something. Basically, there are ten teams in our league, and we all play each other during the regular season to decide which two teams get a berth in the province-wide championship tournament, or the Provincials. The best teams in our league are probably the Mustangs and our biggest rivals, the Bulldogs. If we win enough games in the regular season to end up in first or second, we get to play against the seeds from the central and northern zones for the provincial trophy. Tonight's game could put us into first place above the Bulldogs if we won and establish bragging rights for a few weeks until we played them again. It was huge.

The game was about to start, but I hadn't seen the opposing team's pitcher. I secretly hoped Luke Fabro wasn't going to make it as I warmed up with Zander in the bullpen. But when I stepped on the real mound to take my last tosses, Fabro's Civic pulled up behind the fence in left field, the silver stripe reflecting the sun. He parked it so everyone at the game was forced to notice how expensive his vehicle was. Walking slowly with his typical cocky strut along the fence, and his sunglasses propped on his head, Fabro made sure everyone noticed his triumphant entrance. What a douche.

With four minutes until game time, Fabro stepped on the mound to take ten or so warm-up pitches. He looked good, maybe better than he was last year.

In the first inning, Fabro looked untouchable. The only person to even make contact was Nabbi, who worked until a full count, and then fouled off five or six more. Finally Fabro missed the inside corner and Nabbi took the walk, giving us our first base runner. But he was left stranded on first because Oberg struck out on three pitches, two curveballs, and a fastball that Fabro painted the black with for a called third strike.

Trotting to the mound, I knew I would have to pitch flawlessly to give our team a chance. The first two batters of the game I retired. The two-game rest had really helped my pitching—my fastball was humming, and I was hitting my spots.

My arm was feeling good as their third batter strutted toward the plate. I had been visualizing this moment for over a year. I stared down at Fabro, making eye contact for what I think might've been the first time. As I looked at him closely, I realized his hair was quite dark very close to his scalp. He must dye his hair, I thought as I rubbed up the ball between both palms, holding my mitt in my armpit. What a pretty boy! Fabro held his hand out toward me like a crosswalk guard signalling "time" as he dug toeholds in the batter's box. First the back foot, then the front. Then he adjusted his batting gloves and finished by crossing himself. Yeah right, as if he ever went to church.

After his elaborate routine, the main function of which seemed to be showing the young ladies in the crowd his exceptionally tight pants, I started my wind-up. I gave him a taste of the ol' fastball to start him off. He watched it for strike one. I knew he was a good hitter so I didn't want to give him anything over the heart of the plate, so I went with the fastball again—I have the most control over the fastball. I kept it low and outside. He swung and missed for strike two. I was up on him two strikes and no balls; the thought flashed through my mind that I could be the first one to strike him out in two seasons. At 0 and 2, it was a chess game now. He had had trouble with the fastball so I could go with that, but if he was waiting for it, I was in trouble. The slider was an okay choice, but if it didn't slide, it was just a lollipop waiting to be smashed. I decided to go with the change-up—he was probably waiting on the fastball.

I was wrong. He saw the change-up coming all the way and tattooed it back up the middle, missing my head by inches. I'd committed the worst sin in baseball by letting a batter get a hit on a 0 and 2 count. I slapped myself on the thigh with my glove as he rounded first, and then he tipped his hat to me to, like, say thank you or something. Luckily, I didn't give up any more hits and we got out of the first inning unscathed.

The first half of the game was a real pitchers' duel. We had both given up a few hits here and there, but they were scattered so no one scored. In the bottom of the fourth, my luck changed. Struggling with control, I walked the first batter up, which is a bad thing at any time, but especially when he's the eighth hitter. The ninth batter bunted the first pitch and sent a dribbler down to Randall at third. Randall was caught napping, and when he got to the ball, he booted it into foul territory, allowing the runners to advance to first and third. I was in a jam. Sometimes when I'm in a jam, I forget to pitch smart, and just pitch hard— not a great idea. I leaned back and heaved a fastball at their lead-off man, but he wasn't overpowered. He hit a double that landed on the "R" in right field. When the ball screamed over my head,

I didn't even want to look at it. That scored a run, and put runners on second and third with none out. I called time to take a deep breath and walk around the mound a couple of times. I noticed Luke Fabro was smiling like a serpent in the on-deck circle, waiting to have his crack at me. Once my nerves calmed, I chucked a couple of good ones by their second hitter. I had two strikes on him so I decided to make him chase a fastball high and outside. He chased it, but got the end of his bat on it, blooping it over Nabbi toward Charlton in centre. Both players sprinted hard for the lazy fly ball that looked to be right in the middle of the two of them.

Everyone in the park saw it coming. It was like a hundred other bloopers you see on the highlights at night—two fielders looking up toward the same ball and crashing before it comes down. It was a "yard sale" collision; Nabbi's hat flew off and Charlton lost his glove as they collided and landed on the freshly balded ground, hard. The ball dropped beside them and we all watched helplessly as two more runs scored. Sonya hustled to the ball before the guy could get past second and called time. In the ensuing minutes, both teams' coaches and the umpires went out to check the fallen boys while the crowd murmured in the stands.

From behind me, I heard Fabro speaking in baby-talk to his buddies. "The monkey and the chief fall down and go boom." There was a muffled laugh from the dugout. I couldn't believe what I was hearing.

After a few minutes Nabbi and Charlton both staggered to their feet, obviously shaken up by the collision, and the fans clapped politely.

"Just hit it out to the Indian," Fabro continued. "He looks like he's been drinking a little of his old man's firewater." The snickering died down as soon as their coach got back to the bench, but Fabro was still smiling his I-am-so-superior smile.

I was seething inside. I'd thought I hated Fabro, but after the way he talked about two of my best friends, I absolutely loathed him. I could feel myself shaking on the mound as he stepped into my tunnel vision. He didn't know that I had heard him in the dugout, but I was hoping he could feel my rage as I flexed my jaw muscle over and over. I started my windup, slow and calculated, and gunned a slider high and outside. I didn't want the umpire or Fabro to think I was doing anything other than trying to pitch out of this jam. If I wanted to intentionally bean him, throwing the first pitch at his head would be a sure giveaway. Now that the stage was set, I gripped the ball hard over the seams, preparing for the four-seamed fastball. In my windup, I felt like a coiled cobra ready to pounce. I reached back to throw as hard as I could, fury fuelling the velocity of my arm. Focusing on the blond curl of probably salon-coloured hair that dangled under his chin, I let the high heat fly. I missed his chin, but not by much. Instead, the ball pelted him in the neck just above his shoulder. He went down, limp, like a water balloon dropped from a balcony. For an instant I worried that I had injured him or worse. But that worry quickly turned to the fight or flight instinct as Fabro jumped to his feet and charged the mound.

"I'm gonna f*%$ing kill you, Gunderson!" he yelled as he ran toward me.

I let the fight instinct prevail. "Bring it on, you effing racist . . . duck butt!" His eyes changed from rage to confusion when I said "duck butt," and back to rage again. I really am the worst at speaking under pressure.

He threw a couple of punches that got me in the side of the head and upper back (I was kind of turned away from him because

I don't know how to fight and he, being the hockey player, dropped the gloves all the time). I kicked out a few times with my eyes closed but hit nothing. When I opened them, I saw that the umpire had Luke pinned under him and Coach K. was holding me back. Fabro swore a few more times at me, and I just started saying "Sorry" over and over again, real pleading like. I wanted the ump to think it was an accident.

After the rhubarb, the umpires called the coaches for a meeting. They must have bought my "sorry" routine 'cause they let me stay in the game. Coach K. wasn't even mad. Fabro, on the other hand, was suspended for two games and was forced to leave the vicinity of the ball diamond. I watched with great satisfaction as he got into his car parked outside the left-field fence to watch the rest of the game.

The beanball gave me new energy, and I struck out the next three batters to retire the side.

In the dugout, Coach K. yelled out the batting order and then said, "Okay boys, three runs, three innings. We got this. Dig deep now for me, boys. Let's get on the sticks."

With Fabro not pitching anymore, "getting on the sticks" was a much easier thing to do. The relief pitcher that came in was tired from their game last night. We rocked him all over the diamond like it was batting practice and rallied for five runs. I even got an RBI when I chopped a curveball down the line, knocking in Jiggle. They pulled the first reliever in the sixth and brought in their third-best guy—a submarine-style pitcher without a lot of speed.

His performance was okay until Oberg stepped to the plate with one on and two out. The guy tried to pitch a bunch of junk to him, curveballs, sinkers, a forkball, but nothing was effective. Finally, he tried to sneak an inside, belt-high fastball past the big farm boy.

Oberg opened up his stance and pulled it into deep left. As the ball sailed out of the yard, I looked out at Fabro, who was frantically fumbling with his keys trying to start his car and drive out of the way of the blast. The lights came on just as the ball struck the passenger side window and smashed into his front seat, setting off the car alarm. Oberg started jogging in time to the wailing of the siren, holding back his urge to laugh at the furious Fabro, who was shaking his fist, and a certain digit, in our direction. The rest of the team followed Oberg's example and did some synchronized pelvic thrusts to the beat of Fabro's alarm, causing him to shake even harder.

I pitched shutout ball for the rest of the game and we won 7–3. We now sat alone at the top of the league, and I was leading the league in strikeouts (I did count them every game, but I didn't need a calculator).

As we were joking around in the locker room after the game, I thought, This is the pinnacle, the highest point of my baseball life. I need to enjoy this.

Later, as Jiggle and I walked into the parking lot, Frazier showed up out of nowhere. Even though he was still about ten car-lengths away, he almost made me jump. It was extra weird because Frazier had never come to a game before and nobody in my family had seen him since Dad cut him off. I had been worrying a lot about him in the last couple of weeks. I was starting to envision him sleeping behind a dumpster using a dead cat for a pillow or something.

Jiggle knew that Fraze had moved out and that it was tense at home lately, so he told me he would meet me at the car, leaving me alone. Frazier actually looked good. His hair was cut shorter than usual, and he was smiling his chick-magnet smile as he strode up to me. He gave me a manly half-hug and said, "What's up?" He was a cool guy.

Ever since I was a kid running around under the bleachers looking for dropped change at his basketball games, I've wanted to be like him. Even though he was pretty messed up, I still wanted to be like him. He was laid back and charming, and could always look at things from a different angle than the rest of us. He always said cool things that made you think about life.

One time after my mum took us to church, I was thinking about if God really did exist and if he created the whole world and all the people in it—like my Sunday school teacher said. When I asked my mum if the story was true about Adam and Eve, she said no one could prove it, but if you have faith, God is real to you.

Then Frazier said, "Brook, if you were walking in the desert and you found a watch on the ground, could you imagine that the watch might have spontaneously formed without the aid of a watchmaker?"

"No, I don't think so," I replied.

"What if millions and millions of years went by and all the material for the watch was on the earth, all blowing around. Would there be a chance that the pieces might have come together in the exact way to form the watch?"

"I would say that's impossible."

"I think I agree. That's why I believe there's a watchmaker out there," Frazier said.

It's kind of a stupid story, and I bet he doesn't even remember that day, but that was the kind of stuff Frazier always thinks of.

"Good game, pal," he said to me as I adjusted my hat. "You made some great pitches out there—really hummin' it. It reminded me of myself as a Little Leaguer."

"Thanks. I got pretty lucky a few times out there," I mumbled. I'm not too good with praise.

"And when you beaned that pretentious punk in the neck, man, that was tight," he said.

"Where were you sitting?" I asked. "I didn't see you the whole game."

"In my friend's SUV. He is an ex-Bulldog and wanted to watch his alma mater, and I wanted to come watch my all-star little bro," he said, grabbing the brim of my hat and turning it backwards.

"Thanks for coming," I said, straightening my hat back. I didn't really know what else to say.

"No problem, the pleasure was all mine. Plus I made fifty bucks on a bet too." He reached into his pocket and pulled out a green twenty-dollar bill. "Here, take this, you earned it for me. And uh, don't tell Dad you saw me here, we aren't exactly cool right now." He pulled the brim down on my hat, and gave me the "zip your lip" sign, throwing away the key and all. Sometimes he treats me like a kid.

I wanted to tell him that he should come home, or at least call Mum, but I can never talk to Fraze candidly. I always skirt around the real stuff and keep it superficial.

"No prob, bro, and thanks for the twenty," I said. I looked down into my bag pretending to organize it, while I worked up the courage to ask him the next question.

"So, you doing okay? I mean, have you found a place to live?" I tried to sound nonchalant, but I think it came out a little wobbly.

"Me? Oh yeah, I'm doing good. I'm renting a little room from a guy I work with. It's small compared to the house, and doesn't come with Mum's world-famous banana bread, but it's okay."

Frazier put on his all-is-well face, all smiles and charm. He was probably hoping to put me at ease.

"So you got a job then, eh. That's pretty sweet," I said, feeling relieved. "What are you doing?"

"It just part-time stuff . . . in pharmaceuticals," he said, looking at his watch.

I was about to ask how the heck he was qualified to work in pharmaceuticals, but then I understood. Frazier either really thought I was naïve or secretly wanted me to know what he was into.

"Oh," I said, examining my cleats.

"Hey, it was nice to see ya play, pal. Don't tell Dad anything, okay. You can tell Mum I'm doing good, and not to worry, but I don't want Dad to come searching for me."

He stuck his fist out toward me and I pounded it with my fist, signalling our conversation was over.

"I'll see you around, eh," Frazier called over his shoulder as he jumped into the brand-new SUV that was idling behind us. I couldn't see who was driving because all the windows were tinted dark grey.

I stood in the parking lot alone for a few seconds thinking about Frazier's new job in "pharmaceuticals." I guess a dead-cat pillow wasn't the only thing I had to worry about happening to Frazier.

I snapped out of the trance as the rocks rolled and scratched under Jiggle's truck as he pulled up beside me.

"Hop in, Brook, you're wasting good celebration time," he said.

I threw my bag in the back and climbed into the front seat. Then I just let any thoughts about Frazier be pushed out of my head by the good thoughts about being in first place. Baseball is a lot easier, and more enjoyable, to think about than my brother selling dope.

Nine

MOON SHOT—A home run hit high and far. Also a Ruthian Blast, dinger, tater, four-bagger, yard shot, or round-tripper.

The high of winning made everything funny. A few of us went to get some pizza after the game at a greasy joint in the industrial section of town. Jiggle unscrewed the lid of the spicy pepper flakes that were on the table beside the parmesan, while I was in the can. I fell for the oldest trick in the book when I dumped a half a pound of chilies on my slice. I should have figured something was up when Seth kept staring at me then looking away while I was getting ready to shake it on. I wasn't even mad. I just laughed and tried to shake some chilies in Jiggle's hair.

Seth kept telling everyone at the table that the Bulldogs were lucky that the umpires broke up the fight before he got there because he was going to use some submission hold he learned from his uncle Tony that would have "knocked them unconscious in less than three freakin' seconds." Seth had been one of those eight-year-olds who actually thought he could beat up grown men when he was wearing his Teenage Mutant Ninja Turtles pyjamas.

After the pizza, Jiggle said he had the "ultimate sweet idea," and we should get prepared for the greatest time of our lives. A few of our teammates weren't too excited to be involved in what Jiggle-Me Jason thought was a good time and politely excused themselves. Sonya was one of them; she said, "Good game" to me and then "Goodbye" to the rest of the team. All that was left were Nabbi, Seth, Jiggle, and me.

The four of us drove in concourse to the secret destination. Jiggle and I led the way in his truck, while Seth and Nabbi followed us in Seth's mom's Oldsmobile. (It took much longer than it should have because of Seth's insistence on always maintaining at least a five kilometre cushion below the speed limit.) We drove to the outskirts of the city and followed a winding canyon road deep toward the river. There were no street lights and I didn't see any buildings until we reached the bottom of the canyon. At the bottom there were a couple of big houses being built, still just a skeleton of two-by-fours, and to our right was a parking lot with a mobile home converted to a makeshift clubhouse. I knew where we were now—the new golf course that was scheduled to be finished for the PGA in two years. It cost the taxpayers like a hundred million dollars and destroyed a ton of natural wildlife habitat, but some think it will attract lots of tourism dollars. Frazier is not a fan of the new course. He once wrote a letter to our local MP that only contained the sentence, "I hope the foxes and beavers will be pleased with the boost in our economy when they don't have a home due to the Oasis Canyon golf course and the pleasure needs of the city's wealthy."

Extending straight ahead of the clubhouse was a driving range. It had two parallel fifty-foot-high mesh curtains that were used to stop the balls from landing in the river on one side, and the developing course on the other. The driving range was the only thing that was open to the public so far. The rest of the course was under construction or under huge sprinklers for watering.

Thousands of balls were sprinkled across the dark green grass of the driving range. In the moonlight, it looked like a giant speckled turtle caught in a net.

Jiggle parked his truck behind a pile of sand, out of view of the road.

"If anyone comes down they won't see us," he explained. I knew that meant his plan probably included something not exactly lawful, and I worried a bit about being caught. Not by the cops, they usually just write down your name or call your parents, but by Coach K. I didn't want to think about what he would do.

"What are we doing here?" Seth asked.

"Simple, young Seth." Jiggle was doing his Sherlock Holmes accent. "You see those huge sprinklers over yonder? We shall run and slide on the slippery surface they provide when the water hits the low cut grass on the putting greens."

"But I don't have a swimming suit," Seth whined, always looking to poop on a party.

"Come now, brothers. Let us frolic." While Jiggle was saying the words he was also pulling off his shorts, and I realized there would be more than one full moon out tonight.

Running naked in the moonlight with three other dudes might seem a bit weird to some, but there's something about breaking the rules and being naked at the same time that makes it a glorious experience.

The greens had a two-centimetre film of water coating on the surface of the grass. They were mowed to about half a centimetre thick and were slick as a wet garbage bag, or the yellow tarp we used to play on called the "Slip-n-Slide." I took a ten-step run at a green and then slid the whole way across balancing on my feet like a snowboarder. Nabbi tried to balance too, but fell back onto his butt and slid to the end of the green like a bobsled rider.

"Cool Runnings," I yelled over the sound of the sprinklers.

Jiggle tried a stomach slide and even though he went a long way, he recommended that if we valued our "jewels" we should not try to copy him.

The four of us sprinted from hole to hole, sliding on each green and judging who went the farthest. It was like playing a round of golf, except we were naked, didn't have any clubs, and we were definitely not trying to put balls in the cup.

The course had only about ten holes finished, and I won the distance competition on three. Once Nabbi got the hang of sliding on his feet, he was unstoppable; he won the other seven. Jiggle didn't win any distance competitions but the judges gave him the freestyle award for his creative slide manoeuvres. The best was his "720 spinner," where he did two full spins on his butt with his finger pointing straight up like a disco star from the seventies. Seth stopped participating after I mentioned that there might be a security guard sleeping in the clubhouse. From then on, he stayed close to the car, glancing at every noise he heard, like a paranoid rabbit. Even though we razzed him a bit for being such a baby, I was secretly glad that we had a lookout. I was having a great time, but it was more like the fun a person on a diet has when they go on a Krispy Kreme bender. I would get flashes of guilt and fear when I thought about the consequences of getting caught again, but the fun centre in my brain was flashing at a higher rate than the fear centre. That was why I didn't mind Seth standing guard.

It was a warm night, but after the initial adrenaline burst, we started to get cold. I noticed that Nabbi had goosebumps on his arms and his teeth were chattering like mad. "Suck it up, buttercup," I jokingly said as we walked back to the cars, covering ourselves with our hands.

"My blood is not thick like your Canadian blood," he said. "I am not built for the cold."

Putting gonch back on after you have been wet sucks pretty bad, but I had no choice. Jiggle-Me, on the other hand, had planned the outing and brought a fresh, dry pair of underwear. He was quite pleased with himself as he came striding out from behind the truck in fluorescent green man-panties, which provided hammock-like support up front, and disappeared like dental floss in the back. He gave a little twirl to show off his "manties" just to disgust us.

"Seriously, why would you wear something like that?" I said. "It looks like you're trying to smuggle a budgie in those things."

"I found a great deal at the Salvation Army, and they're surprisingly comfortable to boot," Jiggle-Me Jason said, adjusting the obviously uncomfortable behind portion.

"You mean to say that you are wearing underwear so very close to your, um . . . specials, which may or may not have been worn by a male stripper?" Nabbi asked, looking very concerned. "I heard that strippers have many diseases that they deposit into their underwear."

"Oh yeah, I bet there are more crabs in those gonch than at Red Lobster." Seth was very proud that he came up with such witty joke in such a short time. He looked around at us with this anticipatory smile on his face to see if we were laughing, but we weren't. I was too sickened to laugh, and Jiggle's demeanour changed when Nabbi mentioned the diseases.

He quickly said, "I washed them before I put them on, you idiots," but then he jumped behind the truck and changed back into the wet gonch.

After that, Nabbi and Seth decided to call it a night. They had seen enough of Jiggle-Me Jason to last a good two lifetimes, but more importantly, Seth's mum would kill him if he was late for his eleven o'clock curfew. My curfew would be waived this evening. I had arranged it so I could stay out as long as I wanted. We used to do the old trick where I would tell my parents that I was sleeping at Jason's house, and Jason would tell his parents he was sleeping at my house, but we got busted once when Jiggle's mum called to tell him that he forgot his PJs. Tonight I promised Taylor a ring-pop if she would cover for me. Our usual set-up was this: She would wait until Mum and Dad were in their bedroom, then open the front door and close it again loudly. Then, in an audible voice, she would say something like "Hi Brook, what did you do tonight?" . . . wait for a few seconds . . . "Oh, okay. Good night." Then she would just go to my parents' room and tell them that I was home, but seemed really tired from the game so I just went straight to bed. Taylor was the ultimate confederate, she had total trust from my parents, and she was totally loyal to me. They never questioned her honesty when she said anything so they would never check if I was in bed.

Shivering beside the truck in my under-roos, I told Jiggle that I wasn't ready to go home yet, and he agreed. We sat in his truck with the heat on full blast to get warm for ten minutes until Jiggle-Me grabbed a handful of garbage bags from behind his seat.

All the gates to get directly into the driving range were locked, but we found a spot under the mesh that we could crawl under. I went in first and then pulled the mesh up so Jiggle could shimmy under. He barely made it.

"It's times like this I wish I had a 'six-pack' and not a 'keg,'" he whispered, sucking in his gut.

We glanced toward the clubhouse to make sure there was no light on. He gave me the "flashing pinkie" sign, and we sprinted to the middle of the driving range. It was like we were six again at an Easter egg hunt. I grabbed as many golf balls as I could and stuffed them in a garbage bag like painted eggs. At first, the Pop Rocks were blasting in my stomach because I was waiting to see some rent-a-cop come running out of the clubhouse wielding a sawed-off shotgun and a crazy look in his eye. But after I filled my first bag and no one had shot at us, I calmed down.

I started to work on my second bag when I noticed that Jiggle had already filled three. It looked like he found the jackpot at a part of the field that sloped down like a funnel. I had finished my second bag when Jiggle had finished his fourth and thought, Man, that kid has all kinds of obscure talents. It was actually pretty hard work, gathering up golf balls; we spent at least a good hour doing it and my back was sore.

Jiggle found an easier way out of the mesh wall near the back of the range and we lugged our loot back to the truck, two bags at a time. He started the engine and we drove partway back up the road. Flicking off the lights, Jiggle pulled into a farmer's field above the course. We had to stop and walk about ten minutes through some tall grass until we reached the edge of a cliff that looked over the whole river bottom, including the golf course.

First things first. We both went to the edge of the cliff and unzipped our pants. I don't know why I can't go anywhere elevated without taking a leak. It's like a hardwired male instinct—when standing at a high altitude, urination is a must. I mean, what good is territory if you can't mark it? I made a note to be more careful next time I was under the Calgary Tower.

"Man, it is pretty up here," I said to no one in particular.

"Don't start getting all emo on me, Brook. I brought you here to hit some balls not to make out." Jiggle was holding an old wooden Louisville Slugger in one hand and a bag of golf balls in the other.

It was probably two or three in the morning, and the moon was low in the sky and directly in front of us in the distance. The golf course looked much better from up here. The sand traps and greens looked like a piece of modern art below me. Light green and brown oblong circles pasted on a dark green background. I could see the lights of the city to our left, the yellows mixing with the reds to make an orange hue over downtown. Beyond the fairway, the river slithered and bowed bordering the course like a snake, its scales reflecting the moonlight as it moved.

The crack of the bat shattered the silence like a gunshot. Jiggle had just crushed a golf ball five hundred feet into the river. We froze; if there was a guard down there, he probably heard that.

A minute later, when we figured the coast was clear, Jiggle said, "Throw me some soft toss, Brook."

"Sure," I replied, grabbing a bag of balls.

I moved a few feet to Jiggle's side while he got into his batting stance, facing me, about two metres away. I tossed a few under-hand toward his waist and he smashed them off the cliff. You can hit a golf ball about twice as far as a baseball because they are wound so tight. Jiggle hit about thirty balls into the night, and about five of them cleared the river. Each one had a blue stripe on it with the words "Oasis Canyon Golf Course" written in yellow. I guess they stamp that on them to prevent theft.

Jiggle's bat was a bit heavier than I was used to, so it took me a while to get used to swinging it. On about the fifth toss I got in a rhythm and smashed one that landed in the river. We estimated it was about five hundred feet to the bank—that's like a Mickey Mantle shot if you can make it. It felt good to watch the balls jump off my bat for once. They soared in a massive arc, accelerating until they reached their peak, and then plummeting even faster to the ground. Some of them landed in the mud with a soft thud, others disappeared into the river never to be seen again. The most impressive ones hit the pavement of the parking lot and bounced back up, almost to their original height. Only a handful of all the balls we hit bounced back after their fall.

I pretended for a moment I was in the situation I'd dreamed about since the first time I picked up a bat. The bases are loaded, it's the bottom of the ninth and I'm staring down the pitcher. The championship game is tied, and we need just one run to win. All I need is one little hit and we win, then I'm the hero. I wait for my pitch, when it comes I swing hard, through the ball. Crack. The ball sails over the river and we win the game. It's a far-fetched fantasy because I'm not a very good hitter, and I've never hit very well under pressure, but on the edge of this cliff, I could dream.

We had been there for about two hours, but Jiggle-Me wouldn't leave until he hit the tin roof on the mobile home clubhouse. He'd been trying for about twenty minutes with no luck.

"Dude, let's go. I'm getting tired," I said.

"Just ten more tries, and then we can split," he promised.

It only took him six. The ball drifted high above the driving range and then screamed straight down toward the clubhouse. When it landed on the roof, it sounded like someone shot a cymbal with a shotgun. A light immediately flicked on in the window. We looked at each other for a bewildered moment, then dashed to the truck, leaving the half bag of balls in the grass.

"Holy crap, I bet that guy soiled himself when he heard that!" Jiggle said as we climbed into the truck.

"*I* almost soiled myself, man. That was effing loud!"

Jiggle squealed the tires, and we flew up the canyon toward the city. In the two hours we'd spent on the cliff we'd only used about half a bag of balls; the other five bags were tied tight and rolling around in the box of the truck.

"What are we going to do with five garbage bags of Oasis Canyon golf balls, Jiggle?" I asked as we entered city limits.

"We have one more stop tonight if you're up for it."

"Sure, what you got?"

"I thought of it today when Oberg broke Luke Fabro's window."

We drove back to the Northside and pulled up to a large house with one vehicle parked in the drive, a purple Honda Civic hatchback with a silver stripe and a busted-out window on the passenger's side. We crept out of the truck and hauled the garbage bags to the passenger's side door of Luke Fabro's car. He had taped some clear plastic as a temporary window to keep out the rain. Jiggle carefully ripped a hole in the plastic and slowly poured the first bag of balls into the front seat. The back seat was almost entirely filled with sub-woofers and speakers, not leaving a lot of room for golf balls. By the time he had emptied all five bags, there was a sea of Oasis Canyon golf balls that reached the dashboard.

When I snuck in through the patio door of my house, the darkness of the night was being delicately forced away by an invisible sun behind the mountains. I jumped in bed and laid my exhausted head on the pillow. I lay awake trying not to think about Frazier. I wished he hadn't come to see me today. If this hadn't been the day I found out my brother was dealing drugs, it would have been the best day of my life up to this point. Thankfully, I had other things to think about as I fell asleep. I was envisioning Luke Fabro's face as he opened the door of his precious Civic and was washed over by a wave of golf balls bouncing like a million grasshoppers around his feet.

I fell asleep with a goofy smile on my face.

Ten

AROUND THE HORN—Throwing the ball to each player in the infield, or around the horn, after an out. Used to create energy and team unity.

A ray of sun somehow found a perfect path through the trees, between the bushes outside of my basement window, and past the shades to shine directly on my closed left eyelid. It's like the ghost of my sister's Barbie was getting revenge for the time I melted her face with a magnifying glass and stuck it to Ken's butt until it dried like that. I wished I'd covered my windows with a few layers of black hockey tape, like Frazier did in his room. The guy could sleep all day if Dad didn't pour water on him. Dad used to call Frazier a boomerang kid, because he tossed him out of the house after high school, but he came right back. The way things were going around here, like the constant worried sighs my mum was heaving, and the transformation of cheerful-dad into silent-dad, I was hoping Frazier's boomerang instincts would come back. But it was easier if you just didn't think about it. I have become a world-class ignorer of bad emotions. As soon as a thought, about Frazier and my dad or something, creeps into my mind that might lead to anxiety,

I just daydream about pitching in college someday, or how it might feel to have my picture on the wall of champions. Then it goes away. It's simple, really.

It was Saturday, and I had planned on indulging in an epic sleep-in, but the brightness of the sun had chased the sleep away, and my body thought it was time to wake up. I was glad I woke up when I saw how nice it was outside.

The sun was framed by a pure blue sky and there was not even a breeze. That was the part that amazed me—you only get four, maybe five windless days every summer in southern Alberta. It would be a shame to waste it.

I woke Jiggle up by pressing number 2 on the speed dial. He wasn't very coherent at first, but when I told him I wanted to go "canal skiing," he got excited.

"Sweet idea, bro. I'm gonna call the team, we can make it like a bonding experience," Jiggle said.

I put on some board-shorts and a T-shirt and climbed up the stairs to the main floor. Jiggle would be here in about a half-hour, and there was no use showering since we would be swimming in a canal that contained the runoff from about ten farms and ranches in the area. The best thing to do was just not think about the crap in the water and enjoy good things about the experience. Kinda like life.

I opened the fridge to search for something to fill the void in my stomach, when Taylor tugged on my shirt.

"Hey, man. What's going down?" I said. I always call Taylor "man," it makes her smile.

"Nothing much. I did what you said last night. The rents didn't even have a clue," she said, biting her fingernails as if she was nervous or something.

"Yeah, *muchos gracias*, old fellow. I don't have your ring-pop right now, but I'll bring one home tonight." She laughed at the "old fellow" remark.

"Well, the thing is, Brook, that I don't really want the ring-pop anymore." She was looking out the window when she said it, and then she started speaking at a breakneck pace, like one of those "Some restrictions apply" guys at the end of a radio commercial. "I was hoping instead you would come watch me at my piano recital tonight. I'm playing some really fun things, I bet you'll like it, and there are some older kids in the recital as well and they can play, like, Mozart wicked good. But you don't have to if you have other plans."

"Whoa, Tay. That was some serious speech acrobatics. I would love to come see my superstar sister tickle the ivories. What time does it start?"

"Six. But I don't play till about six-thirty. Really? You really want to come?" She could hardly hide her girlish glee. I love when Taylor gets excited about something, it's like Christmas morning every time.

"Yeah man, I'll be there for sure. You just got to promise me that when you bow or curtsy or whatever at the end you wink at me. Deal?"

"Deal! Oh I'm so excited. I need to go practise," she said and ran into the piano room. Then she stopped and called out, "Brook, I can't wink very good without opening my mouth and wrinkling my face—can I just blink both eyes instead?"

"That would be fine, man," I said, chuckling.

I listened to the songs for a few minutes while I waited for Jiggle-Me to come pick me up. It was nice to have a sister like Taylor who thinks you kick butt even when other people think you're just a skinny punk with a girl's name.

WE'VE BEEN GOING canal skiing as much as weather has permit-
ted since Jiggle got his licence. It is poor-man's waterskiing; nobody
we know owns a boat. Basically, you tie a ski-rope to the back of a
vehicle and then drive on the edge of an irrigation canal pulling a
skier, or in our case a knee boarder, behind you until you get to the
next bridge. The place we go, you can get about a half kilometre
before you have to let go of the rope and turn back around.

It was about fifteen kilometres to the spot, so we all piled in
Jiggle's truck. I sat in the back on one of the lawn chairs, with
Sonya and Seth. Nabbi and Charlton were in the cab with Jiggle.
The wind filled my shirt as we sped down the highway, and for
once in my life, I looked fat. Sonya laughed when I puffed my
cheeks out and crossed my eyes. It was a juvenile joke, I know, but
the wind in the back of the truck was too strong for us to talk so
we had to communicate with gestures. Sonya had to hold her
hair with her hand so it wouldn't fly in her face, but a few strands
wisped around her temples as she smiled. I wished I could freeze
that moment in the back of the Ford on our way to the canal—it
was one of those moments in life when you feel totally content.
It was like the best of my life captured in a snapshot.

We slowed down beside two dirt roads that stretch parallel on
either side of the man-made irrigation canal. The water was about
six feet below the road—still high enough. The farmers had not
needed to drain much yet to water their crops because of the rain
in the spring.

Jiggle parked the truck on the bridge that straddled the canal
below. The first thing we did was tell Sonya to look the other way,
and peed off the bridge. Five streams of urine arched off the bridge
and pitter-pattered into the water below sending ripples in five

perfect circles. Suddenly a sixth stream broke the water on the opposite side of the bridge.

Sonya was hidden from view behind the truck and responded to our obvious surprised laughter with "What? I just wanted to see what the big deal was. Why should you guys have all the fun?"

We have a tradition to see who gets pulled first. Everyone finds a stick of their choice and drops it off the bridge on the up-stream side. Then we run to the other side of the bridge and see whose stick made it under the bridge the fastest. Charlton's stick won that day.

We all stood in our swimming suits on the outside of the barrier that keeps cars from driving off the bridge preparing for the traditional jump. Jiggle counted to three and we all jumped, ripping a white hole in the glass surface of the slow-moving water. I doggy-paddled to the shore, breathing quick short breaths because the water seemed to freeze my lungs. Five years of swimming lessons and as soon as I step in any body of water other than the university pool, I forget the front crawl and relapse to the doggy paddle. At least the sun was hot enough to warm us as soon as we got out of the water.

Charlton was holding the ski handle I bought at a garage sale last summer between his hands, one hand gripped on top, the other underneath. He was lying on the kneeboard, trying to maintain his balance when he yelled, "Hit it" up to Jiggle, who stepped on the gas and pulled him out of the water. It took about fifty metres before Charlton pulled himself up to his knees and started to lean left and right, making "S" shapes behind him in the water.

Sonya had spread out a beach towel on the short grass and was working on her tan. She was wearing a "tankini," which my sister tells me is a cross between a tank top and a bikini. It was sky blue with yellow trim and showed a couple of inches of skin around her midriff. Since she was lying on her stomach, I noticed she had two dimples on the small of her back. I have never met any boys with those dimples (or maybe I've never checked)—I wonder why some girls have them?

When Jiggle-Me Jason was getting ready to go, Nabbi was getting ready to drive, and the rest of us were getting ready to look away before Jiggle came out of the water. He does it every time; he arranges his shorts so that half of his butt is showing in order to give us a surprise "half-moon" when he comes out of the water. He then laughs hysterically all the way to the end of the canal.

Today was no different, but Seth didn't look away quick enough.

"That is re-freakin'-pulsive," Seth hollered at the half-naked Jiggle, and I think he felt a little violated.

THE SUN WAS STILL HIGH in the sky when I got my turn, so the cold water felt good as I tried to balance myself on the kneeboard. I yelled, "Give 'er" to Jiggle and the water pushed against the orange board until I was skimming on top of the greenish canal at thirty kilometres an hour. I pulled myself up on my knees, tugged my board-shorts down over my white skinny thighs, and then made a few cuts out to the edge of the water. I dragged one hand behind me in the water, sending up a rooster-tail spray, and did a few zigzags. My hair was still dry because I hadn't dunked it yet, and it was blowing a bit in the wind. I leaned hard to my left and accelerated out, almost level with the truck. When the bridge got close, I decided to let go while Jiggle turned the truck around. On the way back, I toyed with the idea of doing a three-sixty spin to impress the crowd. It wouldn't be too hard, just pull the rope behind my back, grab it with the other hand and let the truck rotate me around. I twisted the board halfway around a couple of times to get my confidence up. When I saw the people sitting on the shore, I twisted to the left and put the handle behind my back with my left hand. I grabbed it with my right and I started to feel the truck pulling me around. Before I could do anything to correct my angle, the edge of the board dipped under the water and I was yanked under with my arm behind my back. I tried to let go, but the rope was tangled around my wrist and it dragged me under the water with the board acting like a parachute, enhancing the torque on my shoulder. I felt a pop and a sudden surge of pain as my right arm twisted free of the rope and I frantically tried to get my head above water.

When I came up, my friends were laughing, thinking all I did was swallow some grimy canal sludge, but their expressions changed when I gasped, "I think I broke my arm!"

THE EMERGENCY ROOM was empty, except for a dude we know from homeroom who works at a pizza place we go to. He had a bloody towel wrapped around his thumb. "I hope the other half didn't get mistaken for a pepperoni," Jiggle said, trying to cheer me up.

My right arm was literally hanging a couple of inches lower than my left, and I could hardly lift it above my waist. It was not a piercing pain, but more of a dull, throbbing pain centralized in the front portion of my shoulder. When I told the doctor that, she gave me an ice pack and said I would have to get an x-ray before she could tell me anything.

She bent my arm every direction and asked, "Does this hurt," to which I replied yes to almost every angle. I asked if I would be able to pitch in two months for Provincials. She just said that we would have to wait and see.

The thought of not being able to pitch made my bottom lip go soft, but I bit it quickly and my sadness turned to anger. Anger at myself. Why did I have to try to show off like that? What could I have gained from completing a three-sixty turn on an effing garage sale kneeboard? For three hours I sat miserable, in a room that just had curtains for walls, cussing myself out, and wishing I could rewind time. In desperation, I tried praying to the watch-maker to please heal my arm, to put me back together again.

WHEN THE DOCTOR came back I tried to read her face, but she wasn't giving anything away.

"It looks like you have a small tear in one of your four rotator cuff muscles, and some severely torn ligaments, almost clean away from the bone." She said it professionally, without emotion, not like the doctors on the soap operas who always act so moved by their diagnosis.

"How long until I can pitch again?" I asked. I'm sure I looked like a wild man to her, with my eyes bugging out of my head, but I didn't care.

"Injuries like this take a while to heal," she replied.

"How long?" I urged.

"I can only estimate because everyone heals differently, but judging by the severity of the tear, I would say with extensive physio-therapy, you could get 75 percent of your strength back by next year and maybe the rest in another year after that."

"Two years?" I was almost crying now. "Can't we operate or something? I have to pitch in Provincials in two months!"

"I'm sorry. An operation wouldn't get you well any faster than physiotherapy. There's nothing we can do but medicate for the pain." She put my arm in a fabric and Velcro sling and then scribbled something on a pad and said, "Take this to the pharmacy and they'll give you some pain pills. You'll need to come and see me again in three weeks."

I wished she could have prescribed something for the pain that was smouldering from wherever my emotions come from. I bowed my head in my good hand, and I felt the tears pushing on the backs of my eyes. For the first time since the Little League World Series game, I cried. Through blurry tears I looked at the clock on the wall above the yellow curtain. It said 7:13. I had totally missed Taylor's recital. No wonder the nurse said they couldn't get in touch with my parents. Mum and Dad would have had to turn off their cell so as not to disturb all the little pianists.

The thought of my little sis standing in front of a grand piano taller than her, wearing a frilly white dress and perfectly shined black shoes, bowing at the end of her piece and scanning the audience in vain for me to wink at, made me feel even more awful. Worse even than the time I accidentally hit her in the face with a snowball and gave her a fat lip right before school picture day. Every time I walk by the hallway that has all the family pictures hung up, I feel a twinge of remorse when I see Taylor trying painfully to smile with her swollen elephant-man lips in her Grade 2 photo. She was so excited for me to come to the recital too. Man, I wished I could turn back time.

I wiped my tears before Jiggle found me. When he noticed my red eyes, I told him that my arm hurt really bad. I don't think he believed me, but he pretended he did so I wouldn't be embarrassed. The rest of the guys were still in the waiting room reading magazines and watching the ten-inch TV that was mounted in the corner by the ceiling. When I told them what the doctor said to me, everyone got quiet.

They all focused their eyes on the sling when I walked into the waiting room, and I guess they could sense that I was feeling *über* lousy, because Sonya came up to me and tentatively rubbed my good arm. "Don't worry, Brook, you'll figure something out."

Her brown eyes seemed so genuine and concerned that it made me feel like crying again, not because of my arm, but because Sonya had to share in this crappy situation.

FOR THE NEXT FEW DAYS, it seemed that I saw the world through dirt-brown-tinted glasses. I had a knot in my stomach all the time as I ruminated about what an idiot I was. In the span of seven seconds, I had lost any chance I had to pitch in college, and probably the provincial title. I couldn't sleep at night, partly because my shoulder hurt, but more because my inside ached. I had let my team down. I had lost the only thing that made me different from any other kid at school—the only thing that made me feel like me. I did the calculations. If I could get 75 percent of my strength back that meant my fastball would go from eighty miles per hour to sixty. So by next year I might be able to blow a fastball by a ten-year-old from thirty feet.

At school, I moped around wearing the sling, which immobilized my arm. I got tired of telling people what happened so I just started saying I fell off my roof. I had already missed two games; the team won one, and lost the other. It was like torture watching the games on the bleachers.

I decided that I needed to think of a prank. It's the only thing besides baseball that gives me any joy in life. The idea came to me when I was standing at the urinal trying to take a leak. I stood facing the white porcelain, took my stance, and unzipped. But then a dude came into the bathroom and I seized up. Sometimes,

I swear I have the shyest bladder in the world. If somebody is even within a square kilometre of me, I can *not* let it fly. Other times, like if I am on a building, I have no problem.

The dude came in the bathroom, stood beside me, and looked toward the ceiling while he did his business. He finished his whiz, zipped up, washed his hands, and left, all before my little guy overcame his stage fright and liberated a few drops. I walked to the sink to wash my hands and the scheme popped in my head.

The pink hand soap in the bathroom was the exact same colour as my dad's brake-line fluid.

THE NEXT DAY I brought a litre of brake fluid from the garage to school. In the second period, after I asked to go to the washroom, I put my plan in motion. Using a dime to unscrew the plastic knob that opened the soap holder, I removed the refillable bag and poured the soap out into the sink. Then I refilled it with the oily brake fluid. I repeated the process with all the soap dispensers in the main bathroom and then admired my handiwork. Jiggle would be proud, I thought. I didn't include him in this one because I wanted to watch when he tried to wash his hands in pure oil.

The gag worked flawlessly. The water beaded up when people tried to wash their hands and they were pretty freaked out. A few guys tried to get their friends to wash their hands so they could see the reaction when the "soap" didn't rinse off. But I wasn't getting any Pop Rocks in my belly, so I went back to class. It wasn't the same without Jiggle.

Later that day I got a page over the intercom that said I needed to come down to the office. I assumed my mum had left a message for me, probably to tell me that nobody would be home tonight and I should make sure Taylor gets some supper, but when I got there Principal Fisher sat me down and fixed me with a prison-guard stare.

"It has come to our attention that someone has replaced the soap in the main bathroom with brake fluid. You wouldn't know anything about that would you, Mr. Gunderson?" he probed.

"No sir, were the dispensers not coming to a full and complete stop at intersections?" I asked. I felt like being a wise guy. I didn't have baseball anymore, what could he take from me?

"Brook, we have three witnesses that said they saw you coming out of the bathroom holding an empty brake-fluid bottle."

"Oh," I said.

He leaned back in his chair and tapped his temples a few times. "Mr. Gunderson, I expect these things from Mr. Parker, but not you. And to tell you the truth, brake fluid in the soap dispensers isn't what concerns me the most. It's the reports I've received from your teachers of you constantly gazing outside the window and refusing to answer direct questions with anything more than one word. Brook, is something going on in your life that I should know about?"

I wanted to say, How would you like it if one day you woke up and the title of principal was gone, and you couldn't ever be a principal again, and on top of that your older brother is a junkie and a drug dealer, you recently broke your little sister's heart, and your parents are so busy worrying about the drug addict and the perfect child that you become an afterthought at best? Is that enough going on in my life?

But instead I said, "Nope."

Principal Fisher—The Fish—looked across the large oak desk at me and squinted his eyes just a bit, as if he was thinking. Finally he said, "I see. Well, if anything does come up, we're here for you. The counselling services here are top notch."

"I'll be sure to look into that if the need arises, Mr. Fisher. You never know when you might need a top-notch mental heath professional," I said, looking out the window.

He picked up some papers and bounced them on the desk to get them to stack neatly. He had this caring look on his face like he wanted to say something else, but then he swallowed it and returned to the character of The Fish. "Since we don't get much trouble from you, I have decided to give you only a week of detention. Report to Mrs. Chalmers' room at 3:45. Good day, Mr. Gunderson."

I had been to detention plenty before, but I was usually with Jiggle. The D.T. room looked empty, incomplete without my best buddy. The posters on the wall never change. There was one with a kitten hanging by one paw from a tree with a caption that read, *Hang in There!!*

Another one showed a frog in a pelican's mouth, its head already swallowed by the bird, but the frog was still choking the pelican. The caption said, *Never Give Up!*

A third one had a pile of lemons beside a jug of juice. It said, *When life gives you lemons, make lemonade!*

All the posters had the same theme—we know you're all juvenile delinquents, but with a little bit of effort you can do anything. What a load of bull. I used to work every minute of my life to become a great pitcher. If I wasn't on the mound physically, I was there mentally, pondering and visualizing how to deceive the batter. Now I was a nobody, I couldn't strike out my grandma, and she is going blind.

When Mrs. Chalmers was looking the other way, I leaned toward the lemonade poster and wrote in all capitals:

WHAT IF LIFE GIVES YOU DOG CRAP? SHOULD I MAKE A DOO-DOO SHAKE?

Eleven

HOT-BOX—A play in which a runner is stranded between two bases. The fielders toss the ball back and forth, while the runner tries to get to a base. Also called a pickle.

Most of my time for the next few weeks was spent in my bedroom. I blacked out the windows with hockey tape and brought my mum's old record player into my room—it was the only musical device I could move into my bedroom. The Simon and Garfunkel record was the only one in the collection that I recognized, so it spent a lot of time spinning on the deck. It actually wasn't that bad once you got used to it. I would come home from school and head straight downstairs, and then lounge on my bed listening to "Homeward Bound" and "I Am a Rock" until my mum would bring a plate of supper down, or I got hungry enough to make myself something.

I felt ashamed or something. I felt like at school everyone either had no idea who I was or was whispering, "That's the guy who ruined his chance to become somebody."

The huge, spongy, black headphones from 1963 I was wearing drowned out the outside world, so I didn't hear the knock on my door. Paul Simon was crooning away when my dad came through my bedroom door. I could tell he was upset as he stepped over a pile of clothes, topped by the rag that used to be my sling. For some reason I couldn't throw it away. The tool that used to hold up my biggest asset—my arm— was now just a yellowing scrap that smelled like a fat kid's belly button.

"Your brother overdosed today." His words were measured. "He's in stable condition, but unconscious at the hospital."

I didn't know how to act or what to say, so I just sat, looking at my slippers.

"The hospital staff informed me that the overdose was caused by a large amount of cocaine found in your brother's stomach, a result consistent with someone who had 'body-stuffed' a large dose to avoid apprehension by the police."

"Huh?" I said, still looking at my slippers.

"Basically, when a person is carrying a large amount of drugs on the street, usually to sell, they store the narcotics in something that can be held in the mouth, like a balloon. Then, if the police come to make a bust, the dealer will simply swallow the balloon and conceal the evidence. Unfortunately for Frazier, the balloon broke when it was exposed to the acidic environment of the gut and caused an overdose."

I let the information sink in and felt a thick wave of guilt. I probably should have told somebody about Frazier's job in "pharmaceuticals." Maybe I could have prevented it. It was like I was at the bottom of an outhouse and life just kept crapping on me. I was so caught up wallowing in my own pity that I forgot that Frazier was on a far worse path than mine.

I still couldn't find the energy or motivation to say anything, so I just sat.

"Your mother, Taylor, and I are going to visit him if you want to come," he said.

I looked at my feet for a few seconds and slowly wiggled my toes underneath the grey slippers. "Sure, just let me get changed."

We drove to the hospital in silence. I felt bad for my mum again, but felt awful for my dad. Mum looked like she was empty, like her emotional tank was drained and nothing else could come out. But Dad looked like a man swallowed up in guilt, like he was on the brink of sobbing. I was sure that Dad was blaming himself. If he hadn't decided to stop "coddling" Frazier and make him earn his own way, he wouldn't have had to get such an illegal and dangerous job.

In the hospital, a nurse directed us to Frazier's room. He was sleeping when we got there and sleeping when we left. He looked cold, clammy, like a person in a black and white movie. Mum just held his hand and sobbed softly while Dad talked to the health-care team. It is amazing how much my mum loves Fraze, even after all the grief he has caused the family. Thankfully, the doctors told Dad that he would recover with no complications. That seemed to help Dad unclench his shoulder muscles, and he returned to his old demeanour.

When Taylor asked Dad why Frazier did all those drugs, he told her that some people have a greater susceptibility to addictions, and that Frazier was one of the unlucky ones. I shuddered; I didn't want to try my luck with dope or anything else and end up plugged into a feeding tube, eyes fluttering under their lids.

The street lights reflected off the raindrops on the windshield of our car as we drove toward home. In the back seat I was thinking, if there is a watchmaker, why does he let the world suck so much? My mum was miserable, Frazier was slowly destroying all his brain cells, and my future looked like I would never make it back on the mound again. Even Taylor's reflection in the opposite back-seat window looked like she had just eaten something sour. It was too bad that such a smart, good little girl had to be exposed to such a gloom fest.

My dad felt the void in the car and tried to make conversation. He must have sensed that the family needed someone to step in and bring some normalcy back to the situation. He became Doctor Gunderson again.

"Had a patient in today," he said. "I found out from a regular checkup that he has stage four colon cancer." He paused to look at me in the rear view. I just stared at the wipers. "I know the guy fairly well, he's a few years older than me, but I also know that he probably has two years left, tops. The tumour is untreatable. It isn't causing him any trouble, and he probably won't even know he has it for a while. He has a beautiful family and seems happy. The problem is that he doesn't speak any English and his grown daughter comes in to translate for him. The daughter doesn't want to tell him that he has the cancer, so that he can live a normal life for a few years. So I have a question for you, Brook. If you were in my situation, would you tell him about his cancer and risk spoiling the time he has left, or let him live a happy but unaware life?"

"Is he going to die no matter what?" I asked.

"Most probably."

"If he knows about the tumour, will he go through chemotherapy, and be sick and bald for the last months of his life?"

"That's usually the case," my dad replied.

"Then don't tell him," I said. "His daughter is probably right, he'll be better off being happy for as long as possible."

We drove for a while saying nothing. The clicking of the turn signal was the only sound as we exited off the main road. If I were going to die I would rather it just nailed me suddenly—like a fastball to the temple. I would hate to wait around knowing it was going to bust through my door at any second, or not.

"It makes sense to try to help people avoid any hardships," Dad finally replied. "I tried to do that with Frazier for twenty-one years, but in my profession, it's not my place to keep information from anyone. I'm planning on getting a different translator, and telling him tomorrow about the tumour, and his life expectancy."

"Why?" I asked, surprised by my dad's callousness.

"For some people, cancer infects their cells much less than it infects their spirit, making them angry and bitter at the world. But for others, the revelation that their time is expiring is the best thing that ever happened to them. They do the things they always wanted to do but never had made time for. They write novels, compose music, spend time with their loved ones, climb mountains, and generally *live* for the first time while they're dying.

"For some people the news I give them about cancer devastates and destroys their life, for others it enriches it."

"But how do you know which people will bounce back?"

"I don't. Some people have the ability to turn their hardships into strengths, others stay stuck in the mud. But the ones who do get up, well, those are the strong ones."

I knew my dad was trying to teach me something. He was using that tone that he uses when he wants you to figure something out. That's his style. If he wants you to say the word "elephant," he'll tell you about the trunk, the big ears, the thick grey skin, and probably give you some stats about the annual rainfall in their native habitat, but he'll never say the word "elephant." I was pretty sure what he was getting at.

That night, while I fell asleep listening to Paul Simon sing "I'd rather be a hammer than a nail," I silently decided to start physiotherapy. And I think I agree with Mr. Simon. Who would want to wait around until you get whacked, when you can do the whacking and build your own house?

THE SEASON WAS more than three-quarters finished and I hadn't gone to a game since I started physio. I went three times a week in the evening, and so far, all the games conflicted. I didn't mind missing the games, there were too many people there with too many questions, at least in their heads. Lethbridge is a smallish town, and when your brother almost kills himself with an illegal substance, they are not exactly going to let you cut the ribbon at the opening of the newest hunting and fishing boutique. Your family becomes one of those that parents don't want to let their kids become too friendly with. I just avoided public places as best I could so I wouldn't have to think about the people talking about Frazier.

I hadn't seen Jiggle and the guys for a couple of weeks because they'd been busy with the pre-playoff schedule. They slipped in the standings a little and were in second place, behind the Bulldogs.

When Jiggle called to invite me out, I was pumped to do something besides listen to records in my room and play video games. He promised what he had planned would cheer me up. I couldn't wait to see what was turning in his noodle this time.

Jiggle picked me up and we went to Seth's house where Nabbi, Charlton, Mason, and Randall were waiting. Seth's parents weren't home so we had the place to ourselves. When we got there, Jiggle banged his hand on the table like a judge calling for order.

"I guess you are all wondering why I called this meeting," Jiggle said like a CEO. "The project we will be working on this evening is called 'The Hamilton Hop.'"

I assumed that the project name came from the location of Seth's house—on the corner of Hamilton Street. The neighbourhood was a new middle-class subdivision and all the matching houses were packed close together. The roof of one house sloped down to the next roof with only a metre or a metre and a half in between.

Jiggle explained that from his calculations, one could run across the roofs of roughly twenty houses in a row, hopping from one roof to the next. The second to last house on the block had a lower roof, about ten feet to the grass, and could be used as a getaway route into the alley. The plan was all seven of us would climb onto the roof of Seth's house and get in a line. We would then travel down the block across the roofs, jumping from house to house until we reached the "jump down" house, sprint down the alley back to Seth's place, and enjoy the spoils of the prank by repeating the story over and over again until late in the evening. In order for the Hamilton Hop to be successful, the fastest runners needed to be at the back of the line and we all needed to keep together. If the first guy was too far ahead of the last, then the homeowners would hear the footsteps of the first and come out in time to catch the last guy.

Seth was of course not excited. "No freakin' way! My parents will freakin' kill me!"

"Dude, your parents are gone until at least midnight, don't be such a dillweed," Jiggle said.

Jiggle-Me, being the mastermind that he is, had already prepared for Seth's resistance and had taken his glove hostage. He was holding the glove behind his back with a Ziploc bag full of green food colouring in the webbing.

"You get up on the roof with the rest of us, or your glove is a Saint Patrick's Day decoration," Jiggle warned.

Seeing his precious glove in such dire straits, Seth conceded to join in the hop, on one condition—if we got busted, everyone had to testify that we forced him to do it.

THE CLOUDS DIFFUSED the light from the moon and the stars were nonexistent, a good night to pull the stunt off. I must admit that I was a little nervous; it had been a while since I had trespassed. The last time was the winter before, when Jiggle and I climbed the water tower and took a leak off it. He thought it would be cool to make yellow snow from fifty feet.

It was about ten o'clock at night and there weren't many cars on the street. Jiggle put us in the proper order; him and Mason in the front, Charlton and me in the back, and Seth, Nabbi, and Randall in the middle. The street lights were high enough to shine on the tops of the houses, but I could only see until the eleventh house, which was the one with the tallest peak.

Jiggle turned to the rest of us and mouthed the words, "Just follow the Jiggle-man," and then jumped across the first gap onto Seth's neighbour's house. He landed like a water buffalo off a diving board with a huge thud that shook the foundation of the house. Mason echoed him with his size twelves and they scampered up to the peak. Seth didn't want to go, but Nabbi punched him in the kidney, forcing him to daintily step across. The rest followed. When I got up to the edge, the Pop Rocks were boiling and I hesitated for a second before I used my standing long jump skills that I learned in Grade 4 phys. ed. I landed on the edge, barely missing the drainpipe, and reminded myself to jump farther next time. Charlton apparently had a burst of adrenaline because he passed me, running up the shingles to the peak. Now I was the last in the line.

After the first two houses, we got into a rhythm. Climb ten steps up the side, run six steps down the slant, leap across the gap in one fluid motion, and then climb up again. The adrenaline was intoxicating. No one said a word, no one dared. The height and the novelty of being on a roof gave me a feeling of giddy elation, like riding the roller coaster at West Edmonton Mall. Jiggle looked back every once in a while, grinning like a lunatic.

For some reason I thought of that Christmas poem about the night before Christmas. That part where the guy hears such a clatter, then looks out the window to see what was the matter; then on his roof he saw "a miniature sleigh, and eight tiny reindeer." The poor suckers inside must think somebody dropped eight pregnant rhinos on their house as we tromped over their bedrooms, shaking the light fixtures with each frantic step.

The pitch of the next roof was steeper than the rest. We were at house number eleven, more than halfway done. It was much higher than the others. Standing on the peak, I could see all the way across town. I surveyed the park that extended into the blackness of the river bottom about three blocks to our right. I had to be careful not to slip as I shimmied down the other side, reaching the space between the two houses. This gap was the most treacherous of them all. The whole gang was clustered on the edge looking down thirty feet to the flower pots that lined the walkway below. The problem with this gap was that it was not only wider than the others, but the next roof was more than two metres below it.

"We gotta go balls-out to make this jump," Jiggle whispered. "If you go soft at it, you'll have daisies shoved so far up your—"

"We're wasting time, fellas; let's do this already," I interrupted. I figured by then, the people in the first house were probably tearing open the shutters, and pulling back the sash to see what the heck was on their roof.

Nabbi went first and cleared it easily. Then Jiggle and Randall went at the same time—I thought the house was going to cave in. Seth was the next one. He took a run at it but I could tell he was scared because he jumped too far back from the edge. I swear he was going to splat on the cement like a dirty diaper, but his foot caught the edge of the drainpipe, ripping it away from the roof. The noise was ugly. Ugly like a car crash. Lucky for Seth he was able to get onto the roof before the drainpipe swung down and broke the kitchen window below it. I froze. I thought, If I don't move, maybe the people in the house wouldn't notice the busted window.

"Who in the blazes is up there!" a booming voice boomed from the kitchen. "You punks are dead when I catch you!"

I tell you what, if that didn't light a fire in my shorts, I don't know what would. I jumped the gap with three feet to spare and spidermanned up the next house faster than a cat out of a pot of boiling water. The next nine houses were a blur; they could have been hurdles on a track for all I cared. At the last house, I saw the guys jumping off onto the grass in all directions. It was like our ship was on fire and everyone was scrambling to get overboard. When I landed on the grass, I headed straight for the fence and hopped it in one jump. Man, I wish I were that athletic all the time. I landed in the alley and saw three guys running toward the park, two going back toward Seth's place, and a portly figure diving headfirst into a garbage receptacle, sliding the lid over silently. If I had a hat, I would tip it to Jiggle-Me Jason. The kid has got a serious brain on those shoulders. Nobody was going to check in a dumpster for a Hamilton Hopper.

The "you punks are dead" dude was behind us in his truck as we sprinted toward the park. I knew it was his truck because the tires were screeching and it looked like he was on three wheels as he came around the corner. I made brief eye contact. He looked like a maniac with his brow bent in a perfect V behind the steering wheel. I wished I could run like this in games; I was effing hauling!

He was gaining on us, and at the rate he was going I worried he was going to run me over. I assessed the situation and realized that we had the advantage because we were on foot. I yelped up to Nabbi and Seth to follow me, and then took a sharp right into the nicely kept yard of a beige house. We raced into the backyard, leaped the fences of three houses in a row, and came out on a completely new street—away from the rampaging dude. The park was only one block away, so we made a beeline toward it; at least there were no street lights in the park and if we needed to we could keep going into the river bottom.

Without the maniac on our heels, I felt how tired my legs were. We slowed to a jog as we entered the park; the street was a safe football field's distance away. We crept noiselessly through the green strip until we were hidden in the middle of a big hollow concrete tube that the kids play in on the playground.

"It smells like the children urinate often in this dome," Nabbi said.

"Yeah the freakin' brats freakin' whiz all over this place," Seth replied. His voice was high-pitched, like he was really scared or hiding something.

That was when I noticed the big symmetrical stain on Seth's crotch. "You whizzed yourself!" I said, a little too loud, pointing to his wet jeans.

Nabbi got this grossed-out look on his face and darted out of the cylinder. I flew out the other side and we all ended up beside the swing set.

"I couldn't freakin' control it, guys. It just gushed out when the guy yelled out his broken window." Seth's words were pleading, like a little kid who broke his mum's vase.

I kind of felt bad for the guy so I told him that one time I did that too, back when I hit a cop car with an egg on Halloween. It wasn't true but at least it helped Seth calm down.

We barely started whispering about what we were going to do next when the truck came flying down the street and *into* the park. Its headlights bounced up to the sky and then back down, shining on the slide beside us, as it hopped over the curb. Grass was ripping up and flying behind his Goodyears as he floored it toward us. The sight scared me so much that I didn't even stop running as my bladder involuntarily let loose. So much for my shy bladder, I thought, as I reached the edge of the park and jumped the chain-link fence into the tall grass. Nabbi and Seth were on my tail, I heard their footsteps behind mine, and a whimper as Seth breathed. The path we were on quickly led to a steep slope that ended at the river bottom. My goal was to get down into the heavy cover of the trees—we could hide down there.

It was hard to see the ruts, and the terrain changed before my eyes could instruct my feet to watch out. I slipped on some loose rocks and fell on my butt. I started to slide down the hill like a tobogganer, picking up way too much speed. Digging my heels into the dry grass was useless—they wouldn't hold—as I accelerated toward the river bottom.

At the bottom of the hill was a little drop-off that landed in a bunch of bushes. I slid off the drop-off like a person coming off the waterslide, and plunged into the middle of a thousand scratchy twigs. A couple of seconds later Seth and Nabbi landed nearby, judging from the sound of branches breaking.

"Pissssst." I pushed air between my teeth.

Nothing.

"Caw, caw." The bird impression ought to get them.

Still nothing.

"Mooooo."

"Why are you acting like a bovine?" Nabbi grabbed my ankle from below and startled me.

When I bent down, I saw that the bushes had grown in a way that made a leafy ceiling about three feet above the ground. I crawled under with Nabbi and saw Seth, white as a mime with an expression like one too.

"Dude, we're safe. Nobody is gonna find us down here. This river bottom is like ten kilometres long. They'd have to send the dogs." I was trying to sound reassuring, but the mention of dogs made me think of an image we saw on TV of police dogs mauling a drug dealer. The dealer's arm muscle was dangling below his elbow like a slab of steak after the K-9 sniffed him out.

"We're freakin' dead! We are all freakin' dead!" Seth was panicking now.

"Easy, pal. Take it easy, we broke a window, we didn't kill the Pope. I got a plan," I said, thinking of a plan.

I knew that from this side of the river there were two paths that led back up the hill to the west side of town. The problem with those paths was, if somebody wanted to catch you he would just wait on the trail. I reasoned that the only way we could make it back to Seth's was to wade across the river to the opposite side, the Southside, and then take a bus back over the river.

I told the boys my plan and Nabbi was excited.

"What an adventure we are having this evening," he said, his white teeth glowing in the dark.

Seth was okay with the plan, anything to distance himself from the angry dude.

We slowly made our way toward the sound of the water through the heavy brush and trees. Branches were tearing my legs up, gouging and scraping as we plodded along. I wished I hadn't worn shorts.

Seth was right behind me and I sensed he was not as scared anymore, maybe even enjoying the adventure. I held a branch in front of my chest as I walked forward, clearing the path for myself. When I sensed the time was right, I let it spring back and it nailed Seth in the neck. The temptation was too strong.

"Ouch! Freak me!" Seth yelped. "You meant to do that."

"Sorry, buddy, I didn't realize you were so close," I lied.

This kind of stuff is definitely my thing. The adrenaline pumping through my veins, the Pop Rocks exploding, the running, the hiding; this is my medicine, my addiction. I even forgot about my busted arm and Frazier for a couple hours.

When we reached the water, everything was much more visible. The moon was trying to poke out through the clouds to reflect off the water, and I could see the lights of the city across the river. Luckily, we hadn't had much rain, so the water was low. We walked downstream for a few minutes looking for the lowest place to cross. When we found a place that looked to be waist high, I went in.

The water felt icy as it came up to my crotch. I instinctively tried to hold my jewels up out of the water. I was happy that the river would wash away the urine that thankfully nobody noticed. I reached back and grabbed Nabbi's hand, and he grabbed Seth's. We crossed the river like a group of kindergarteners out on a field trip to the museum. We decided it would be safer that way, mostly for Seth, but I don't mind holding a guy's hand as long as he doesn't try to interlock fingers with me.

On the other side of the river, we wrung out our wet clothes and prepared for the long hike up the hill back to civilization. It took about an hour to climb to the top and when we got there our pants were almost dry. We waited at the bus stop looking like homeless people who hadn't had a bath in a month. Seth's jeans were ripped, Nabbi had a huge gash on his elbow that he incurred during the "dry mountain luge," and my legs looked like I tried to fight twenty tomcats, and got whupped.

As the bus crossed the river I said to the boys, "We should get off a few stops before Seth's place and then walk one at a time back to the house. Seth can go first, then Nabbi, you wait ten minutes before following him. If anyone is out there they'll be looking for a group of three, not a single pedestrian."

I pulled the cord and the bell rang, signalling for a stop. The bus lurched to a halt and made that air brakes sound.

"The bus flatulated," Nabbi said, giggling. He doesn't often make jokes, but when he does, they aren't usually all that witty.

I gave him a courtesy laugh and reminded Seth not to look suspicious as he headed toward Hamilton Street. After ten minutes, Nabbi went the same way and I was left sitting under the street lamp alone. I moved out of the light, thinking that it might be safer to stay in the shadows. Every set of headlights made me tense. They must be the guy or the guy's friends looking for us. My heart thumped faster as I heard the engine of each vehicle coming in my direction. After what seemed to be an hour, I tilted my watch toward the light and saw that ten minutes had gone by. I started my walk slowly with my hands in my pockets, I even tried to whistle to make it look like I really was innocent, but I can only make noise from sucking in, so I gave up on the whistling. As I got closer to Seth's place, I noticed a cop car cruising slowly by.

Must be a coincidence, I told myself. When I turned down the street, I saw two other police vehicles patrolling Hamilton Street, slowly, like two sharks circling a boat. I clinched my stomach and walked as if I was just a curious schoolboy.

A blue and white car pulled up slowly beside me, keeping pace with my walk. I glanced over to him and it looked like he was talking on his radio.

"Excuse me," the young cop said, through his rolled-down window. "Can I talk to you for a minute?" He continued to roll at my pace.

"Sure, what's up?" I said far too casually.

"We're looking for a group of three to ten boys that were involved in some attempted break-ins tonight." He stared at me, no doubt trying to judge my reaction. "You wouldn't know anything about that would you?"

"Break-ins, ossiffer? I mean officer." Man, why can't I talk under pressure? "I wouldn't know anything about something like that."

"Where have you been tonight?" he asked as he stopped the car by the curb.

"Oh, me? Well, I was . . . uh, over at my girlfriend Sonya's house just watching a movie." When I'm nervous, I just grab the first thing that pops in my head.

"What's your name?"

"Gwinn Dumont," I answered with no hesitation. One thing I always have prepared is a pseudonym for an occasion just like this. The real Gwinn Dumont plays third base for the Bulldogs. I try not to smile whenever I think of the time the cops called Gwinn Dumont's house after I got busted for dropping jack-o'-lanterns off the overpass.

"Your girlfriend give you those?" he asked, pointing to all the scrapes on my legs.

"These? No sir, we were playing baseball this afternoon and I got these sliding into second." Not a bad lie, not a great one either.

"What team you play for?"

"West High Mustangs," I replied, although technically I didn't play anymore.

"No kidding eh, I heard you guys got a chance at winning Provincials this year," the cop said. His countenance had totally changed now. He seemed like a big baseball fan.

"We'll have to play well, but we got a chance," I replied.

"Well, I better not keep you up too late. If you see any punks around, you let us know," he said, and then put his car in gear.

"Will do," I said over the engine as he drove to the end of the street.

When I walked in the front door of Seth's house, I heard Seth telling the story to the rest of the guys. Judging from the mood in the room everyone must've got off scot-free.

". . . I was gonna flip him the freakin' bird, but all of a sudden I was sliding down the hill, and then, boom, we were hiding in some bushes. I was like 'this is the freakin' most awesome thing ever!'"

What a knucklehead.

Twelve

GLASS ARM—A reference to a pitcher who often gets arm injuries.
Also a sore throwing or pitching arm.

One of the best things about physiotherapy is the magazines.
I usually tried to get there a little early so I could read the *Sports
Illustrated,* and if nobody else was in the waiting room, I liked to
look at all the hotties in *Seventeen* magazine. Today I had the sports
mag on the outside of the chick magazine. I didn't want anybody
to see me reading the article "What's your romance IQ?"

I took the quiz and scored a seven out of a possible fifty. How
was I supposed to know that asking your date to pop zits on your
back was classified as "non-romantic"? I thought that might be an
expression of intimacy or something. It took me four years of
knowing Jiggle-Me Jason before I asked him to pop my "backne."

I flipped pages for a while, past the "most embarrassing
moments" and "cute skirts for spring" and stopped to skim the
article "How to send the vibe to your crush." I found out that
when a girl laughs at your jokes it could mean she digs you. And
if she ignores your jokes, it could also mean that she digs you.
I guess it is pretty complicated, dealing with girls. If she wants you

to hold her hand in a movie, she will put it out on her thigh—in a prime clasping location. And if she wants to kiss you, she will make sure you see her applying ChapStick to her lips. What a load of crap. I'm glad I don't have any time for girls and their over-ChapSticked lips.

"Brook Gunderson?" the new lady with the clipboard called out, looking around as if the lone skinny young man in the waiting room wasn't what she had pictured in her mind when she read my name.

"That's me," I replied, trying to let her feel my disgust with the tone of my voice.

"Madame Borschak is ready for you now." She gestured for me to follow her back to the area with the rooms separated by blue curtains. "You can bring the magazine with you if you want. You'll have some time to read during the ultrasound."

"Sure. Thanks." When she turned around, I slipped the *Seventeen* onto the desk and took the sports magazine in with me.

Madame Borschak, my physiotherapist, was a firm, stout lady in her sixties, about five-foot-three with defined neck and forearm muscles, which I guess developed from many years of rock climbing. She had all her keys linked through a carabiner on her belt loop, and posters all over the office of sinewy women hanging off cliffs and mountains with only a climbing rope between them and sure death. She was a great lady, real nice, but I am always intimidated by a woman who can grow a better moustache than me. She also had a haircut the boys and I call a "she-mullet." It's basically your regular mullet, long in the back, short on top, but the women's version is usually neatly spiked on top and a bit wavy in the back. She was looking sporty today in her neon pink and black track suit, unzipped at the top to show her "Run for the Cure" T-shirt.

Madame Borschak did the usual things when I sat down. She checked my range of motion with a few stretching exercises. I almost had my whole range back. We did some strength tests—she held my arm back and I pushed against it at different angles. I felt pretty strong. She told me I was progressing faster than was anticipated. It had been about a month and a half since the accident, and the pain had completely disappeared. For one brief second I entertained the thought of being able to pitch again this year, but then reality socked me in the eye like a sockeye salmon; I could only throw about half-speed.

When she spread the blue gel on my shoulder for the ultrasound, I got goosebumps. She rubbed the cool metal end of the ultrasound machine around in circles while telling me the sound waves produced microscopic vibrations in the muscles to increase circulation and healing. I nodded and acted interested, but I really just liked the massage and the chance to read my magazine.

The baseball photos gave me a tinge of excitement and sadness all at once. I used to think I had a shot at someday becoming the guy in the photos, eyes intensely focused on the catcher's mitt, short chin hairs glistening in the sun. Now I supposed the best I could do would be to coach Little League or something. I still had a good pitcher's mind, just not the arm.

I flipped through the magazine looking for something to read. An article on steroid use in the pros showed five of the best long-ball hitters in the Majors swinging the stick. Each picture had a bodybuilder who had admitted to using 'roids superimposed on the shot beside the hitters. The similarities were not hard to miss—both had bulging veins, bulging biceps, and a crazy look in their eyes. I wondered if the juice could help me become a fast-baller again.

The next few pages talked about the NFL pre-season, and I flipped right by. I was not going to waste any mental energy reading about the NFL when it was still baseball season. I was about to close the mag when a little snippet caught my eye. It was only one column long and it was titled "Floating it by 'em." The red print on a yellow background covered a story about a college pitcher named Dylan McCollum who had the second-lowest earned run average in his league, and he only threw fifty-five miles per hour!

Dylan McCollum won't blow it by you with a 90 mph cut fastball. He won't even trick you with curveballs and change-ups. In fact, you'll know what pitch is coming every time: The knuckleball. It floats in the air like a beach ball just saying "I dare you to hit me." Hitters across the league lament facing McCollum, and it shows in their measly .169 batting average against him. When the 5 foot 5 lefthander tosses his nasty knuckler, the hitter goes through three phases.

1) Holy crap, look at that beach ball, I'm gonna clobber this.
2) Holy crap, that thing is dancing like a butterfly in a hurricane.
3) Holy crap, I just missed that pitch by two feet.

The batters are not the only ones who have trouble with McCollum's knuckleball. His catcher had to buy a new catcher's mitt that is 3 inches longer and wider just to be able to stop the ball. Although the new mitt has reduced past-balls, he still missed about 8 pitches a game on account of their unpredictability. "I just aim in the direction of the strike-zone and hope it doesn't float too much; most of the time I don't know where they are going," McCollum told reporters last week at the state tournament. He may not know where his pitches are headed, but he does know where they can take him. McCollum just signed with the Texas Rangers and it is rumored that he could crack the starting line-up in as little as half the season.

I didn't know if it was the ultrasounds bouncing around in my body or what, but the instant I finished the article I felt amazing. I had never been high, but I imagined this was what it would feel like. All the tension in my gut dissolved, my lower back muscles relaxed for the first time since the accident, and I felt like kissing Madame Borschak.

Thankfully, I refrained from smooching Madame B and the inch-long hair coming out of her mole. Instead, I just jumped off the table and said, "Sorry, I gotta run . . . um diarrhea." It happened again, I just said the first thing that flashed into my mind, but the good Madame seemed like a lady who was no stranger to diarrhea. I instantly regretted thinking about her on the can, and immediately tried to push that mental image out of my head as I ran the five blocks to my house.

IN THE HOUSE, I was barely able to control my excitement. I could hardly stand how long it took our computer to boot up, even though it was only about twenty seconds. I typed into the search bar on the internet: "How to throw a knuckleball." The search produced tons of hits. I read as many as I could, and made a mental summary of the instructions: The ball is not held with the knuckles but with the fingertips. You throw it the same way you pitch a fastball, but keep your wrist stable to eliminate as much spin as possible. At the last moment, you extend your fingers pushing the ball away. The goal is to make the ball have no spin so that the air currents can catch the seams and float it in random directions.

We had an old foam mattress that we used sometimes if visitors slept at our place. I hauled it out to the backyard not caring that the dirt was smearing the bottom. I propped it up against the fence and counted off sixty feet and six inches to mark my makeshift mound. I have collected about ten regulation baseballs in my life and I placed them all in a bucket beside me. Now it was time to try my knuckleball out.

I threw the first ten balls and they all looked like slow fastballs with a lot of spin. The next ten were the same. After sixty pitches, I think that one spun slower than the rest, but I could have been seeing things. Each pitch hit the mattress with a *thud*, and then dropped to the grass; I collected them and did it over and over again, each time reciting the steps from the internet in my mind. I didn't know if I was seeing progress, but I didn't care. I would have done anything to be able to pitch again.

There were two weeks left until our last road trip of the season, to Medicine Hat. After the tournament in Medicine Hat, Provincials would start. If all went as planned, I would have mastered the knuckler by then and could try it out in the tournament—that way nobody from our league would see it. Then if it worked well, Coach could save me and use me as a surprise weapon in Provincials. It was a perfect plan. Now all I had to do was learn how to throw it.

The thought of the measly two weeks to learn a very difficult pitch was a potent motivator. I threw bucket after bucket of balls until my arm started to ache. When I felt that steady smouldering in my shoulder, like someone had injected it with jalapeño oil, I slowed down.

After almost an hour of tossing, I started collecting the balls from around the mattress, making sure to lift the handle with my left hand, when Taylor came into the backyard. It was rare for anyone to come into the backyard except to mow it, so I was a little surprised.

"Brook, you're smiling! If I just ruined Mum's guest mattress I sure wouldn't be smiling. What are you so happy about? Why are you using Mum's mattress to throw balls at? Where did you get all those balls? Why are you smiling?" Taylor sometimes has a habit of asking more than one question at a time.

"None of your bizz-natch, twerp." I said it teasingly, still smiling. After all, I really was happy. "I got bored of living in my room, okay."

"Well, I guess I won't tell if you'll watch the movie I rented with me. It's so scary and none of my friends will watch it with me." Taylor loves to rent horror movies even though she misses most of the film because she plugs her ears and covers her head with a blanket when the music gets creepy.

"Fine. You got yourself a deal," I said. "Why did you come back here in the first place?" I asked.

"Oh yeah, the phone's for you. It's Frazier. He wanted to talk to Mum, but she isn't home, so he asked for you."

"What does he want?" I asked, the smile wiped off my face. I hadn't spoken to Frazier since before he almost killed himself swallowing a balloon of cocaine to avoid a prison sentence. Since then, I knew he had left the hospital, but I didn't know where he was staying.

"I don't know, just go answer it," Taylor said, examining the mud smeared on the bottom of the mattress

I walked into the house and stepped up to the counter where the phone was sitting off the hook. I grabbed a pen and started to doodle on a piece of paper before I said, "Hello."

"Hey Brook, what's up? You doing okay?" His voice sounded different, more raspy.

"Yeah, I'm good. You?" It was weird to talk to him. It was like since he O.D.'d he'd become this figurine made of porcelain that could break at any time if I said or thought the wrong thing. It didn't feel like I was talking to my brother.

"Life is good, little bro. I'll probably be coming back home soon, I just need to borrow some dough from Mum. Could you leave a message for her to call me?"

"Sure," I said and started to think about all the other times Fraze had borrowed money from my parents. "What's your number?"

He gave me the cellphone number he could be reached at, and I jotted down the number on the paper I was doodling on and left a note for Mum.

"Okay, anything else?" I asked, trying to be cool even though I was feeling strangely awkward talking to my own brother.

"Um, nope. That should do it," he said. "You take care of our little sister, okay?"

"Yup."

"All right, see ya later."

"Bye."

The chance that the money Frazier wanted was for groceries was slim. He probably owed somebody something or needed a fix. My gut felt like someone had put a stick in it and started to turn it until all my insides were wrapped tightly, like an elastic band twisted on a toy propeller. Even though I hated what Frazier was doing, I was too immobilized by my status as younger brother to do anything.

Plus, he was a smart, headstrong person—what could I say or do anyway? Thankfully, I had my mattress and my knuckleball to occupy my mind. I returned to the yard and recited the internet rules and threw knuckleballs until I had pushed Frazier out of my mind.

My ALARM CLOCK RANG at 5:00 a.m., and I wasn't even tempted to hit the snooze button. I hardly slept because visions of knuckle-balls kept dancing in my head all night. Every morning for the past week, I'd given myself two hours before school to throw knuckle-balls against the mattress, then I would throw again after dinner. This morning the sun was hidden behind the grey clouds, and the rain had been coming down all night.

The rain soaked through my long-sleeve shirt and I felt a bit chilly at first, but by the fifth bucket, I was warm enough to throw without blowing into my cupped hands each time.

A drop of water slid down from the crown of my head, and it dripped off my bangs in front of my eyes. These are the times when I feel most motivated to work hard. I like to push through the pain, to ignore the cold. It was as if I was one of those inspirational stories where the athlete practises every day without any shoes or in a snow-storm. I visualized pitching in the provincial title—my triumphant return to high school baseball. That was the fuel for my fire.

Water splashed in all directions as the ball slapped against the muddy mattress. So far, I had put in seven full days of throwing in the morning and six full evenings—one good week. The repetition had destroyed my mum's guest bed. There was a concave circle in the middle, around where the strike zone would be. At least I was throwing strikes. As of today, I could throw about three good slow-spinning knuckleballs out of the ten in the bucket. One more week of this practice schedule and maybe I would be ready for the Medicine Hat tournament.

ROAD TRIPS make a guy brave.

We got out early from last period to get on the road early. Coach wanted a chance to see the diamond before it got dark. This tournament would be the last chance to sharpen up our skills before the big dance—the Provincials, which would be held next weekend. This was the first time I had been a part of the team since the famous kneeboarding mishap, and almost exactly two weeks since I read the knuckleball article in the physiotherapist's office.

When we got to the diamond, the team went through a short workout to get used to the infield. I didn't participate. I hadn't told anyone about my plan, except Coach K., not even Jiggle. Coach told me that if we were winning by a lot of runs he would give me an inning to pitch, but he couldn't promise anything. That was good enough for me; I just needed a shot. I think Coach felt bad for me—I had only played in two games the whole season.

After our short practice, everybody decided to take a walk around downtown to look for a place to eat. We all decided on a small dirty-looking restaurant called Uncle Billy's Buffet, which advertised "7.99 all-you-can-eat chili dogs." We talked about doing a dine and dash but our waitress was way too nice so we stayed and paid; we even left a tip.

We walked around the city for a while, trying to look for girls. On a road trip, a lot of guys think they're going to find some chick who wants to make out with them just because they're in a different city than their own. We saw a few good-looking girls outside of the 7-Eleven, but we were all too afraid to talk to them, so we just walked by.

At one point we saw a tall woman about four blocks away. She was wearing a short skirt and a tight top that showed her muscled belly. We all stared, mesmerized by the way she swung her hips. We could tell she was too old for us at two blocks, but we kept checking her out anyway. Once she got to the corner of the block we were standing on, I noticed her hands.

"Man hands, dude!" I whispered to Jiggle.

As she approached, we could clearly see the large Adam's apple and a very hairy upper lip.

"Good evening, boys," she/he said, in the voice of a beer commercial announcer, the bass resonating in our heads.

"That chick was a freakin' dude," Seth said with a laugh, before the person was out of earshot.

I punched him in the kidneys and told him to keep his pie-hole shut.

"Yeah. Talk about good from far, but far from good," Jiggle said.

On the way back to the hotel, I realized that the all-you-can-eat chili dogs were trying to make a comeback, and I hurried back to our room, squeezing my cheeks as I ran.

While I was trying to calm the violent seas of my stomach in the bathroom, Jiggle-Me Jason was finding a male mannequin in a dumpster. He was so excited to show me his find that he bounced into our room and practically screamed, "Dude, I found a freakin' mannequin, dude! Think of all the rad stuff we could do with a full-sized mannequin!"

"If you're thinking of cuddling with that thing, you can count me out," I said, just to mess with him.

"Don't be a moron, Brook," he spat back. "We could plant it in the hot tub, or tie it to the bus, or put him in bed with Coach K.

Think of the people's reactions when they see a mannequin being dragged behind a bus!"

"Um, Jiggle, that sounds pretty lame," I said, even though I thought it would be sweet. I was a little worried that any prank could ruin my chances to pitch, especially since I had come so far.

"What!" Jiggle was stunned. "Brook Wayburn Gunderson. I have known you for a bunch of years, and never have I known you to be the type of person who would think tying a mannequin behind a city bus to be lame . . . never." Jiggle-Me Jason was acting like a fire-and-brimstone preacher standing behind his pulpit. "Frankly, I am astonished and bewildered. Yes, that is the word for it, bewildered. In fact, I feel like some kind of bewildered beast— a bewilderbeast."

Jiggle's melodramatic speech cracked me up, so I decided to come clean with my best friend. "It's just that I'm worried that if Coach K. busts me for anything more, I won't get a chance to play again."

"What are you talking about? I thought your arm was just dangling from the socket like a bratwurst?"

"Well, I can't throw the ball very hard, but I've been working on a knuckleball. I mean, I have almost missed the whole season . . . can't we just wait two more weeks until the season is over before we do anything crazy?"

Jiggle paused to take in this new information and to come up with a persuasive argument.

"Wow Brook, that's good news about the knuckleball. And I understand where you're coming from about Kobrinsky, I really do. However, you fail to see some important factors. First, how often do you have the great fortune of discovering a full-sized mannequin? Not often, my friend. To waste this opportunity is like throwing away a chili cheese dog outside a soup kitchen—it would be unethical. Secondly, sure you've missed some of the baseball season, but think of how much of the prank season you've missed. In my opinion, you can't afford to miss this one. And number three, I can personally give you the foolproof, 100 percent money-back, Jiggle-Me Jason Parker guarantee that we won't get busted. Coach K. has a tournament coaches' meeting right now until late, so no worries. Brook, it's the foolproof, 100 percent money-back, Jiggle-Me Jason Parker guarantee. You *know* you can trust that."

I had to smile at my best buddy. He really knew how to weaken my defences. In the back of my mind I was thinking about all the good times I had missed with my friends because I was glooming it up in my bedroom. I really missed being with them and the giddy feeling of almost getting caught. I knew that Jiggle-Me was no slouch when it came to avoiding consequences, and that he was right about Kobrinsky's meeting, but that wasn't the reason I said, "I'm in." And it wasn't peer pressure either. Peer pressure is like something is pushing or forcing you to do something. This was more like a peer vacuum, gently pulling me in. I could have resisted, if I'd wanted to. But I didn't really want to.

"I'm in, as long as you do everything in your power to get me off on the slim chance we get busted. Even if it means taking the fall for me," I said.

"That is no problem. You deserve an insurance policy. Now let's get brainstorming." Jiggle was smiling like he just won the lottery.

After a short discussion, we decided that tying Bartholomew (that was the name we gave our mannequin) to a bus would be too hard to pull off. The drivers watched their vehicles too closely, and they were never parked for long enough. Instead we started by buying a pair of pants and an old shirt and tie for him at a second-hand clothing shop.

Bartholomew looked good in his corduroys and plaid shirt. The only thing he needed now was a hat to cover his flesh-coloured head. Charlton found a beauty—a long-billed, red duck-hunting hat complete with earflaps.

We transported the dressed-up Bartholomew into the elevator and descended to the underground parking area. Jiggle walked unassumingly back and forth in front of the freight elevator waiting for someone to come out. Charlton and I hid behind a minivan with Bartholomew. The freight elevator was the only one that went all the way to the roof of our thirty-floor hotel, but regular guests don't get the key to access it. We waited for twenty minutes until two waiters came down the elevator transporting a crate of alcohol. When they walked out of the elevator and their backs were turned, Jiggle deftly stuck his foot in the doors, holding them open a crack until the waiters disappeared through a storage door. He beckoned to us with the flashing pinkie, and we came out from the shade of the minivan and slipped into the freight elevator.

The bell dinged when we reached the floor labelled "R," and the shiny doors parted, revealing a well-lit all-concrete room. At the end of the room was a ladder that was made of bars lodged directly into the wall leading to a small square hatch marked "ROOF." It was creepy and exciting walking across the bare room and then climbing up the ladder to the hatch. The hatch opened directly skyward, and we all climbed out onto the pebbled roof.

The wind made me sway and I took off my hat so it wouldn't blow away. I walked to the edge and had to resist the temptation to take a leak; there were a lot of people walking below. Jiggle,

Charlton, and I stood on the edge for a while, staring down at the people walking in and out of the clubs, oblivious to our scrutinizing eyes. It was weird, I was standing two hundred feet from a sure death, but I felt calm, I felt happy, I felt excited.

I really couldn't believe I was going to go through with this plan so close to Provincials, but like I said, road trips make a guy brave. Besides, Coach K.'s tournament coaches' meeting probably meant he was getting sloshed.

Jiggle propped Bartholomew up on the edge of the roof and held on to his ankles, steadying him in the crosswind.

"I can't take this no more," Jiggle yelled over the edge toward the sidewalk below. "I'm gonna jump, I swear it! I'm gonna jump!"

A small crowd gathered under the hotel, craning their necks to see the suicidal mannequin above. From where they were, Bartholomew looked like a messed-up duck hunter, teetering on the edge of sanity and a hotel. Jiggle's plan was to wait long enough for a crowd to gather, but not long enough for the cops to come.

"Give me some room, you bunch of A-holes," Jiggle yelled in a desperate tone. "I'm doing it!" The crowd, which had increased to about fifty people, moved back to avoid becoming the victim of a thirty-storey belly flop.

It had been about three minutes since Bartholomew stepped to the ledge, and the crowd was now up to roughly a hundred people. Some of the more drunk people were chanting, "Jump! Jump! Jump!"

Jiggle smiled at us and shoved the mannequin in the back. It fell in an unnatural end-over-end fashion as the crowd let out a massive, collective gasp. When he landed on the pavement, he shattered into a few pieces; one arm flew toward a group of bar girls and they screamed in horror, thinking it was actually an arm. We watched the bedlam for a few seconds and then booked it back to the hatch and climbed down into the concrete room. Jiggle pressed the button for the seventh floor; if we went to the basement, we would run the risk of meeting the cops.

We got off the elevator and ran past the mirrors on the wall to the emergency stairwell at the other end of the hall. Our rooms were on the fourth floor and I barely touched a step on the three flights down, I just held the handrails and swung myself from the top to the bottom of each staircase.

Once safely inside our room, we crowded around the window and watched the effect of the splattered mannequin. The cops— about five cars full—had arrived and were interviewing some of the bystanders. A Japanese couple were taking a picture with the busted Bartholomew, both making peace signs with their fingers.

"If I was thinking straight," said Jiggle, "we could have video-taped the whole thing and made a movie." His eyes lit up and he added, "For future generations of Mustangs!"

I was just hoping we wouldn't end up on a tape of *America's Most Wanted*. The boys in blue looked pretty miffed. I mean, I've been caught by teachers, principals, the mailman, and even the occasional librarian who didn't appreciate the relocating of pictures of topless indigenous African ladies into random religious books, but I have never been hauled downtown to the police station. I don't even know why the cops showed up, we just dropped an old mannequin off a roof. Nobody got hurt; it was basically just a littering offence. At least that was what I kept telling myself as I watched two officers meticulously moving from group to group interviewing everyone who was left. I actually got pretty worked up about it, but I kept it inside because Jiggle and Charlton were having a good laugh at the whole situation. I just sat on the bed thinking about all the bad things that would happen if the cops figured out who did it—and not being able to pitch this year was near the bottom of the list. Pitching again was a long shot, I had accepted that, but I didn't even want to think about what it would do to Mum if her next boy got put in the slammer for mannequin-slaughter after her oldest swallowed coke and almost fried his brain like an egg on a skillet. My mum was too fragile for that kind of back-to-back news.

I slowly stepped to the window with Jiggle and Charlton and peered down at the scene. One police officer pointed up to the roof while he was talking to his partner, jotted something down in his notepad then looked straight at us in the window. I couldn't tell because the street light didn't give a lot of light, but it seemed like we were making eye contact. Jiggle must have thought the same thing because he grabbed each of the off-white curtains and flung them over the window with both hands. Instinctively, Charlton and Jiggle-Me dove out of sight onto the nearest queen-sized mattress, laughing like two-year-olds when you say "poopie."

"You freakin' idiots!" I said. "That cop will *never* consider three teens that suspiciously jump out of sight when he looks at them to be suspects." The sarcasm in my voice must have come through loud and clear because Jiggle stopped laughing and looked up at me with a surprised expression.

"Whoa, dude. Who took a dump in your Frosted Mini-Wheats this morning? I mean seriously, I thought we were all having a good time here," he said. I didn't say anything because I was feeling a little embarrassed at my outburst. I was having fun until the police showed up. Jiggle sensed what was wrong, and said, "Hey man, don't worry about the fuzz. There is no way they could finger us cause nobody could see us on the roof. Hey, and if you want, we can get an alibi. You know, somewhere we could say we were at the time of the drop. It's all good, Brook. We'll be fine. Besides, Charlton and I will take all the heat on the off chance that something happens. Don't worry, you're gold, my man." His tone was very convincing, with a hint of concern.

I looked at Charlton to see if he was willing to take the heat for me, and his soft eyes and nervous smile seemed to say that he would. He knew my family couldn't take much more delinquency. I guess it is nice to have friends that would be willing to do that for you, but it was also a reminder that everyone knew about Frazier and was treating me as some kind of charity case.

I opened the window again and looked down at the crowd and police, both of which were slowly dissipating. "Thanks, guys," I said. "Sorry I flipped out, just a little on edge I guess. It's been a while since I tossed a fully clothed mannequin off a hotel roof." I was smiling again, and most of the worry had melted away.

"Well, we might as well go to Seth's room to watch the Blue Jays' game, eh Brook? Wakefield will be pitching his knuckler for the Sox. We might want to see that, no?" Jiggle said, and winked at me.

He was still keeping my secret, which I appreciated because I wasn't sure I could even throw a knuckleball in a game, and I didn't even know if Coach K. would let me in to try.

"Sounds good," I said, as I grabbed our room key and put my hat on backward. "I would rather mess up Seth's room anyways."

Thirteen

PAPILLON—The knuckleball. Papillon is French for butterfly. The knuckler is thrown at a slow speed with as little rotation as possible, giving the appearance of a ball fluttering like a butterfly.

The first game of the tournament was my first game back. My uniform smelled worse than three months ago. The bacteria obviously hadn't been practising safe sex—they had multiplied big time. I guess I should have washed it, but I didn't think I would need it again.

This tournament had a weird rule. To make sure all the players were wearing proper protection, an umpire came to the dugout with an aluminum bat and gave everyone a "cup-check." We all lined up with our feet apart and the umpire tapped each of us in the groin area. If you heard a "knock knock," you could play, if you heard a "thud thud," you didn't care that you weren't allowed to play. I watched intently as the ump made his way down the line to Sonya—I never really thought about if girls had to wear a cup. The umpire looked ultra-uncomfortable as he got to the only female in the tournament.

Sonya could sense the awkwardness of the situation when the ump kept pulling on his chin stubble. "I can do it myself, if you want," she offered. The ump was visibly relieved and handed over the Easton. We were all surprised to hear the familiar "knock knock"; I guess girls do wear a jock.'

"What?" Sonya said in an overly surprised tone. "You think that *your* bits and pieces are the only kind worth protecting?" she asked the line of ballplayers with gaping jaws. "Not like the human race could sustain itself if your tadpoles had no place to swim."

We all kind of stared in silence for a torturous moment until Jiggle broke the stillness. "I don't mean to be rude or anything, Sonya, but I thought that you didn't . . . you know . . . care about the propagation of the human species . . . at least in the traditional sense."

Sonya just laughed. "What do you mean, in the 'traditional sense'?" she prodded, making the situation even more awkward.

"It's not like any of us care," Jiggle said nodding to the rest of us. "You know, at school, the people say . . . about your orientation." He separated the last word into its syllables like a first grader reading it for the first time.

Sonya laughed pretty hard, squinting her pretty brown eyes as she covered her mouth with both hands. Apparently, she found the whole situation comical. "You guys believe that crap about me and my or-i-en-ta-tion?"

"You mean it's not true?" I butted in.

"Of course, it's not true. The girl who started that rumour was jealous because I get to hang out with the baseball studs all the time. That, and I called her 'uni-brow' in seventh grade before she started to pluck the caterpillars she had for eyebrows. Man, I had no idea *you guys* believed that too!" She furrowed her brow for a moment as if looking back in time and said, "But that would explain why you guys didn't care when I walked into the change room after we beat the Bulldogs, and most of you had your gonch pulled up your butt-cracks like a thong and were singing 'Heal the World.'"

"But why didn't you stop the rumour from spreading?" I asked.

"What do I care about what a bunch of wanna-be pop-tarts think? Let them say what they want to say, no skin off my nose. Besides, I would much rather chill with you guys than a bunch of over-emo girls."

We all relaxed a bit. It seemed like a decent argument.

"Now that I've come out of the straight-closet, let's go win us a ballgame," she said as she underhanded a ball to Jiggle.

I was dumbfounded. A new sensation filled my chest. Why did this new info change anything? Why was my stomach doing somersaults? Why did I notice that Sonya had a small dimple on her left cheek that you could see when she clenched her jaw?

THE GAME WAS an easy win, 8 to 4. Highlights included an Oberg three-run shot in the fourth, Nabbi's diving grab of a line drive up the middle, and a big play at the plate in which Zander got run over. He was blocking the plate and looking out toward right field, when a base runner barrelled down the third-base line. He caught the ball just as the runner laid his shoulder into his chest protector. Zander caught some big air and landed on his shoulders and neck, skidding to a stop on his back. Everyone thought he was uncon-scious until he slowly reached into his mitt and, for dramatic effect, pushed the ball feebly skyward causing the crowd to erupt and the umpire to yell, "You're outa there!" For good measure, Zander "crossed" himself by drawing the curved outline of the stitches of a baseball on his chest; he says it brings good luck.

After the game, we all put our hands in the middle to cheer for the other team. I noticed Sonya's tanned hand was resting on mine. It was dusty from the infield dirt and she had short, bitten nails like mine. Why I noticed it today when I had never noticed before kind of scared me. It wasn't like I liked the girl.

The cheer we did depended on the name of the other team. These guys were named the Spartans.

"One, two, three, Spartans!" we chanted together, yelling as gruffly as we could, and then shook hands with the other team. I told most of them "Good game" but mixed in a few "Great jobs" to keep it fresh.

That night at the hotel, there was a knock at the door of our room. Two police officers stood in the doorway. One was a short man, and the other was a regular-sized woman who looked pretty tall in comparison to her partner. The first thing I thought of, besides "I am a dead man," and "I wonder if anyone's heart has *actually* pounded through their chest wall," was a social studies lesson I'd had about Napoleon. The teacher told us that good old Bonaparte had "small man's syndrome," which means because he was small, he had to overcompensate for his feelings of inferiority by conquering other nations in battle. Maybe this short cop got picked on at school so now he needed to feel tough with his pistol.

We played it cool at first—well, at least Jiggle did. I sat down in one of those never-used chairs by the phone and opened up our complimentary Gideon's Bible, as if it was the most natural thing to do when being visited by officers of the law. Yeah, not so cool. I flipped through the beginning of the book, Genesis, and pretended to be genuinely concerned about who begat whom while actually being concerned about if this cop was going to send me to the pokey in a striped suit.

They wanted to know if we had anything to do with the taste-less disregard for human life displayed last night with the mocking of the serious social problem of suicide. Jiggle just acted super indignant about it, saying things like "Well I never," and "I am ashamed to be numbered with the youth of today. No respect for anything."

"I agree. The term respect don't mean much to your generation, do it?" the short cop said. I expected him to spit on the carpet after he said it, judging from his tone. He only needed a black hat, some chaps, and a moustache and he would be a perfect fit for the role of tough-guy sheriff on an old western—well, maybe if he grew about another foot. Then he locked his viper glare on me while I cowered behind the good book, hoping it might save me from juvi-court. "You there, Billy Bible Thumper, stand up a second, will ya."

My pants were frozen to the chair.

"You got a hearing problem, or a respect problem there, church mouse?"

Still frozen.

"We just want to talk to you. Stand up and we can have a conversation." It was the woman. She was a little less scary than the short-man-syndrome dude, but only by about a micrometre.

I slowly stood up and stood beside Jiggle-Me. I held my hands over my crotch as if I was protecting myself from some forthcoming bodily attack. I don't know why I do it, but whenever I'm in a confrontational situation, I always cover the pickle and jujubes. Must be instinct.

"So, can you two gentleman account for your whereabouts between 8:30 and 8:45 on the eve of the twenty-first of June?" The short cop said this formally, holding a notebook in his hand.

"The eve of the twenty-first of June? Is that the night *before* the twenty-first of June? Like Christmas Eve is the night before Christmas? I'm not sure what you mean, officer," Jiggle said in this overly innocent voice. I could tell he was being cheeky, but it seemed to confuse the short cop for a second.

"The *evening* of the twenty-first of June was last night," he responded, then got a little hot tempered with my best friend. "Look, let's not play any more games, Chico. We have a report from a witness that saw three male teens, one chubby"—he paused to look Jiggle up and down—"one tall and skinny"—now he looked at me. I tried to crouch a bit—"and one dark skinned, enter the freight elevator at around 8:30 last night."

The only thing I could think of was "So much for the fool-proof, 100 percent money-back, Jiggle-Me Jason Parker guarantee." We were totally busted, and my life and my family would be wrecked even more. But I didn't have much time to lament my situation because Jiggle got into character for one of his speeches.

"Oh, I see what this is. It's a classic case of 'Who stole the chocolate almonds we were supposed to sell to raise money for the Heart and Stroke Foundation? Let's just blame the fat kid.' It's the story of my short life. Who cheated on the test? Blame the fat kid. Who covered the steps leading to the drama room with olive oil and caused Ms. Hathorn to twist her ankle? Blame the fat kid. Who tossed a mannequin off the roof? Blame me. Is that what's going on—discrimination based on body mass? I think yes.

"The fact you are calling me both a suspect *and* overweight is hurtful and unnecessary." Jiggle was acting even more indignant and looked about to cry. "Did you know, Officer . . . Officer . . . ?"

"Quinn. Officer Quinn," the short cop said. He was caught off guard and his face seemed to soften as Jiggle went on.

"Did you know, Officer Quinn, that we chubby children suffer much worse fates than just being the first out in dodge ball and getting the odd 'wide load' sign being stuck on our pants? We are statistically more likely to suffer from mood disorders and more likely to miss school on account of bullying." Jiggle paused to wipe a non-existent tear from his eye and continued, "Drawing attention to our unfortunate genetic condition by calling us chubby, as you just did, Officer Quinn, has been known to send us into bouts of deep depression leading to suicidal thoughts.

"So, I don't know about how police work is done here in Medicine Hat, but where I'm from, where the chief of police is my father, Captain Douglas McAlister"—Jiggle had met Captain McAlister a year earlier after an old lady called in about disturbing the peace when Jiggle was using firecrackers to "dispose" of his old textbooks—"we don't perpetuate stereotypical ideas about delinquency such as 'all fat kids have no morals.'"

Officer Quinn was looking surprised and flustered as he took his hat off, rubbed his buzz cut, and put the hat back on. "We're not saying that overweight individuals have no morals, we just want to do our job here."

"Well, you said it, and that is just how I feel," Jiggle said, and ran into the hotel bathroom, slamming the door behind him and letting out audible sobs.

That just left me and the cops. Jiggle had done a great job, his acting was superb. Now I just had to finish them off . . . if I only knew how.

The woman cop spoke next. "I'm sorry about your friend. Will he be okay?"

"Yeah, he'll be fine, he just hates being accused of things he didn't do," I said.

"Well, if you could just give us an alibi, we'll keep on checking the other rooms. You still haven't said what you were doing last night."

"Well, we were watching the Blue Jays' game here in the room, but that doesn't really help I suppose . . . unless . . ." I rubbed my chin as if I was thinking. "Nah, that wouldn't work," I said out loud.

"Try us," Shorty said.

I had a stroke of genius. "You guys wouldn't take the word of a ten-year-old girl, would you?"

"Well, ten-year-old girls don't usually lie to the police. Why, what are you thinking?"

"Just a second," I said, and went to the phone on the desk with the orange light on it, and dialled long distance to my house.

Luckily, Taylor picked up. "Hey, sis," I said into the mouthpiece.

"Hi, Brook! Are you calling me long distance?" she said excitedly.

"Yup, still in Medicine Hat. Hey, I'm just here with some police people and they want to know if I *really* was helping you with your math homework over the phone last night starting around eight."

There was a pause on her end for a second and then she understood. "Oh Brook, are you in big doo-doo this time?"

"It's no big deal, I'm not in trouble or anything, I just want you to answer their questions." I was pretty sure that Taylor knew I needed her to lie me out of this, and I knew she could do it. She was a smart kid. "Will you talk to them for me about studying math together last night?" I was confident that I had given her enough information to ad-lib a story, but not sounding too obvious to the cops, who could hear my side of the conversation.

"Okay, Brook, but I'm a little nervous."

"Don't worry, Officer Quinn is a very nice fellow."

I handed the phone over to Officer Quinn and he started talking. "So, you were on the phone with your brother from 8:30 until 9:00?" I couldn't hear her answers through the phone, so I was sweating it out a little bit.

"What kind of math were you working on?" Quinn knew that the first thing you do to flush out a liar is to ask for details, because the person might hesitate.

"Fractions, eh? Those were tough for me too," he said, but I thought he should have said "Those are still tough for me" or "I never passed a math class in my life."

After forty seconds of mild interrogation, he hung up and discussed it with his partner in muffled tones.

After what felt like as long as it takes Seth to tell his mum every detail of his day when he calls her at night (which is a long time), Officer Quinn said "Goodbye" and "We're sorry for the inconvenience."

They fell for it, hook, line, and fishing rod, and moved down the corridor knocking on each door. I waited until they were off our floor and went straight out and spent all my meal money on gummy worms, fuzzy peaches, a poster of a pony running beside a stream, and stickers for Taylor. I didn't even care that I would go hungry for a day, Taylor had saved my scrawny hide, again.

THAT NIGHT Jiggle, Zander, and I took a soak in the hot tub. When we got there, Oberg was already there, a little tipsy from the wine coolers he bought. They didn't even ID him on account of his five o'clock shadow.

Oberg has washboard abs and was making his pecs dance to the tune of the bar mitzvah song. "*Hava nagila, hava nagila. Hava nagila venismecha*," he sang as his pecs flexed and relaxed. I was a bit envious, truth be told. I stayed under the water as much as I could, I didn't want the guys to notice my skinny white ribs. I even felt a bit sorry for him. He doesn't have a real friend in the world, and I think he masks his low self-esteem by acting overconfident. If he would just try to be nice sometimes, instead of always walking around, chest out, being an arse, he might be a decent guy. He is so busy putting on the I'm-such-a-ripped-tough-guy act, that nobody has seen the real Oberg. It's hard to like a person you're not sure you have ever met.

We had the whole pool area to ourselves. Just the four of us sat, arms up on the edge of the hot tub, talking about baseball, girls, and the Bartholomew gag. There was a sign on the wall behind the teal-coloured plank they called a diving board that read:

WELCOME TO OUR

OOL.

Notice there is no "P" in our pool.

Please help us keep it that way.

The sign made me want to jump in there and take a leak, but I didn't because I heard that some pools put a chemical in that turns bright red when it reacts with urine.

"Well, I think I've had enough," Jiggle-Me remarked to no one in particular. "I feel like a won-ton in a hot soup, all marinated and shrivelled up."

I should have seen it coming. After eight years of being Jiggle's best friend, I should have known that he would walk up the steps of the hot tub with his shorts down, white cheeks a-jiggling.

"Dude, that is so old!" I shouted as I covered my eyes.

"Oh. Were my pants down?" Jiggle responded, sweet as a Girl Guide selling cookies. "Please forgive my rudeness, I am ever so 'em-bare-assed.'"

Oberg grabbed a wet towel and chased Jiggle around the pool trying to snap him on the bare skin. He looked pretty ticked off. Jiggle was squealing and running in little steps like you have to do when you're on a wet surface to avoid slipping on your face. The towel finally nailed him on the back of the calf and a welt instantly formed. Oberg was satisfied with the shot and had mercy on him, telling Jiggle he never wanted to have to look at his bare buttocks again. Jiggle gave him his word as he massaged his purple calf.

That incident put a damper on the mood, so we all went back to our rooms and hit the sack. We had two games the next day, and if we were winning big, I might get my shot to throw the knuckler.

As I drifted to sleep, my mind switched back and forth from pitching to Sonya. I thought about how laid-back she was, how shiny her hair was, how the uniform hugged her athletic frame. And she spit! A lovely, attractive, witty girl who knew how to hock a loogie. Girls like this don't come around every day.

OUR FIRST GAME was in the morning. The chalk lines were fresh and the infield was flawlessly raked. Since I got the mattress, I hadn't played catch with a real person who threw back. Jiggle and I played catch, but I didn't throw the knuckleball. I wanted to surprise everybody.

"The arm feels okay?" Jiggle asked.

"Not too bad. I don't have the heater anymore, but at least I can chuck a bit." I knew I would probably sit out this game because the team we were playing was the northern Alberta champions out of Edmonton—the Kodiaks. They looked good, all big boys, and they could hit. We needed to scout them well because there was a possibility we would meet them in the provincial tournament next weekend.

Sitting on the bench made the game creep by. We were losing and nobody was talking in the dugout. Even Jiggle didn't have anything to say. By the seventh inning, we were down 10–5. Far enough to make a comeback unlikely, but too close to let me pitch. I looked down at Coach K. and nodded my head toward the mound. He just shook his head and mouthed the words "Not yet."

THE BAD NEWS was we lost. The good news was we lost, so we only had one game left and no chance to win the tournament, which meant I would get a chance to pitch next game. We had two hours to get something to eat and be back at the ballpark for warm-up. You never get much time between games when you're on the losers' bracket. Most of the team walked across the road from our hotel to McDonald's for a quick bite.

"I'll have the combo number four," I said to the kid in the orange cap behind the counter. "Can I get that circumcised?" It's a lame joke I always pull when I come to Micky-D's.

"Sure, combo number four—super-sized," the kid said.

Nobody ever notices the slip of the tongue except the people with me. Sonya thought it was pretty funny; she kept laughing after each word as she tried to order the McChicken with an apple pie.

I love those apple pies too, except for when they burn your tongue.

There were hardly any seats left as I panned the establishment with my eyes. Sonya noticed some people leaving and pointed to one of those half-circle booths in the corner. It still had portions of someone's toasted kaiser bun and a drop of that Mac sauce which mysteriously tastes like Thousand Island salad dressing on the table, but we just wiped it the best we could and sat down.

"Hey guys, I got a general question for ya." It was Jiggle, and he looked as if he was concentrating on something pretty hard. "Would you rather have to put your whole head into an elephant's butt, to like, find your keys or something, or eat a hamburger that was made entirely by stacking all the short hairs from off the bars of soap at an old folks home?"

"Dude!" I almost choked on my hamburger. "Why would you bring something like that up? I mean, we were having a nice meal and everything, man! Now I got to think about my grandpa's armpit hair."

"No. It's just a question, a straightforward question that I would like to know your opinion concerning. Sonya, what would you rather do?" Jiggle said. I was amazed at how he could continue to pretend he was serious. Sonya had been holding her napkin up to her face and laughing silently, but so hard that she was bouncing and her eyes were watering. I think she had something in her mouth still.

After she swallowed and composed herself she said, "What are you talking about? I'd just get a new key cut. There's no chance of me swimming in the sphincter of a pachyderm."

"You can't do that. You have to pick one or the other, no changing the scenario."

I laughed at Jiggle's annoyance and said, "Well, what would you do, smart guy?"

"For me it's a no-brainer. I'm getting on a stool and putting my head into the massive poop-chute. No way am I eating soapy grandma hair. Besides, I could get some swimming goggles, a cap, and a nose plug, and probably find my keys, no sweat."

I was disgusted, but it made me laugh. So hard, in fact, that I started to feel a bit embarrassed about my lack of control and how big my mouth must have seemed to bystanders.

"Okay, seriously, we are stopping this conversation right now, I want to eat my fries," Sonya said.

"Yeah, thanks a bunch, numb-nuts. I'll probably hurl if I have to eat the rest of this burger because of your bath-time horror stories of the elderly," I said, pushing my half-eaten burger away.

"If you're not gonna chomp 'er down, send 'er over," Jiggle said with a smile, grabbing my burger. "Can't let this go to waste, can we?"

I finally realized why Jiggle had brought up such a nasty topic while we were eating. It was all in the name of extra food. It didn't bother me that much because it cracked me up and took away any tension that I would have felt sitting with Sonya. Plus, I got to watch her laugh.

I changed the subject to baseball and the fact that even though we lost in this tournament, it didn't matter because we were still in the Provincials next weekend. Just as I was about to say something about going into the tournament as the second seed from the south wouldn't hurt us too bad, because all the teams were pretty even, Sonya interrupted me.

"Brook, do you support the actions of Greenpeace?"

I was totally baffled by the question because, one, it came totally out of left field, and two, I knew that Greenpeace was a famous environmental group, but I had no idea about their recent actions.

"Uhh. Do I support Greenpeace?" I echoed. She had this mischievous grin on her face that made her eyes kind of twinkle, like when a Christmas light reflects off a glass ball ornament. Maybe it was a trick question. "I suppose I support Greenpeace and their said actions."

"Oh, I was just wondering because your teeth are currently supporting a green piece of lettuce. So I wasn't sure."

I instinctively raised my hand over my mouth and although I should have been mortified, the way Sonya's eyes were sparkling when she laughed at her joke and grabbed my free arm made me feel like I didn't need to be embarrassed. She shook my arm and said, like we had been best friends for twenty years, "It's no biggy, we all support green piece now and again, just thought you would like to know."

She had cast some kind of spell on me that made even a slight ribbing seem like a compliment coming from her. It was the best I ever felt with food stuck in my teeth in public.

It was the last inning in our last game in Medicine Hat, and I was more nervous than I could ever remember when Coach called my name to start warming up. The whole team was surprised, but they figured that because this game didn't mean anything, and we were up by five, Coach was giving me some charity for the bad luck I'd had this year. As I walked out to the mound, I wasn't sure myself that it wasn't charity.

"Great to have you back, Gunner," Zander said through his catcher's mask in the traditional pre-inning pow-wow. "You gonna bring the heat tonight?"

"Not exactly," I replied. "But don't worry about the signs. I only have one pitch now. I am sorta gonna be a straight knuckleball pitcher from now on." There, I said it. I had sealed my destiny. I had to commit to this now, no going back (not like I could if I wanted to).

"Sweet, bro," Zander said. "Let's see you make it dance."

Zander jogged back to behind the plate and I was left on the mound. When the ump yelled "Play," I noticed my palms were sweating. Why is this such a big deal? I thought. It's just a stupid game. But somewhere, not in the part of my brain that I think with, I knew that pitching for me was more than a game—it is who I am. If I failed here tonight, I thought, it would open the floodgates of failure for a long time in the future.

I dug my fingertips deep into the stitches of the ball, making a claw. When I stepped toward home plate, I extended my fingers and steadied my wrist. The ball flew toward Zander, spinning forward like a Little League fastball and bounced off the plate. Ball one.

The next one, same thing. Only this time it hit the mitt outside of the strike zone. The batter had this cocky grin on his face, like "Why are you even trying to throw that garbage?"

This time I dug my fingernails deep into the seams and tried to push the ball out hard with my fingers as I released. The result was beautiful. The ball was frozen; I could still read the writing as it floated toward the catcher, dancing and bobbing like a giant snowflake in the breeze. Zander held his glove out to catch it, but at the last second, it floated over his mitt and hit him right in the chest. Strike one! A strike never felt so good before. I figured the secret was to dig my nails into the stitches, that way the ball was anchored until I pushed it away. The batter swung at the next pitch. It didn't float as well as the last one, but it did the job. He hit it, but feebly in the air to Nabbi, who made an easy catch.

I relaxed my neck a bit. When I am concentrating really hard, I always cock my neck slightly to the left. Dad says it's lucky I don't concentrate very often because I would have a crooked spine if I did.

The next batter rocked a bad knuckler into left field for a single; it didn't float at all. That put him on first. I noticed the hitters really take hard cuts at it, like they want to clobber it.

I concentrated on every part of my mechanics for the next hitter, and it worked. The ball was dancing like a ping-pong ball in an electric fan. He missed the first two pitches, to put me ahead 0 and 2. The next one he hit on the ground to Sonya, who rolled the double play to end the inning, and the game.

The next few minutes were a blur of high-fives and butt slaps. I couldn't believe that I was back pitching, and I was good! I might not strike many people out, but my knuckleball was effective.

Sonya said, "Attakid, Gunner. I knew you'd figure something out."

"Uh . . . Thanks . . . you," was the reply that came out.

Coach gave a post-game talk. Something about "You got to believe" and "We're on the way to the big dance and aren't gonna take no prisoners." I wasn't even annoyed with the cheesiness of it; I just sat there with a perma-grin.

Fourteen

WALK-OFF HOME RUN—A game-ending home run. The walk-off derives from the fact that the victims of such a hit will often walk off the field, seemingly in disgust or despair.

Countdown to the Provincials: five days. School was out for the summer, only a few exams to go, and I spent most of my extra study time playing catch with my mattress. Exam week has always been a good week for me. You don't have to go to school unless you have an exam, and since my parents seem to never be home to monitor my studying it's practically a vacation.

When I discovered that digging my nails into the stitches helped the knuckleball float, I did something drastic. I clipped my nails on my right hand to a sharp triangular point. It looked a bit vampire-ish but my knuckler improved big-time, so I dealt with stares at school and my nails getting caught in cotton fabrics.

The only thing that was weird about being home for the week was that Frazier had moved back in while I was away. Well, it was not so much weird as it was awkward. That was part of the reason I stayed in the backyard with my mattress. I guess I was being a bit immature, but I just couldn't look at him without thinking about the overdose. And it wasn't like I felt ashamed or anything, but it was like . . . different now, clumsy. I don't know if he thought I was judging him or embarrassed when I saw him, so I tried to act normal, like old times, but when I listened to myself speak it always sounded like one of those guys that own the local carpet store and make their own advertisements. You know, artificial. We had had a few conversations, but nothing about anything besides the weather, or baseball, or Taylor's latest success, like her perfect report card. Frazier even hinted at the topic of the drugs and his problem, but that was when I got really uncomfortable and changed the subject, or suddenly remembered that I had something to do. I didn't really know why I couldn't talk about it. It was like when I wanted to let Coach's pitch hit me, but my body wouldn't let it happen. It was just easier to avoid the situation altogether.

AFTER PRACTICE, SETH suggested that we all go to the early show to build team unity before the big weekend. Seth really wanted to go see this new summer blockbuster based on a comic book. Almost everyone on the team said they could make it, and we decided to meet at the mall at seven.

When Jiggle and I pulled up, we could hardly find a place to park. It looked like the movie was going to be packed. Inside the mall, everyone was waiting for us in their coolest summertime fashions. Sonya had on flared jeans and a yellow T-shirt that said "Radiohead" on it. I think she was wearing some makeup, but I couldn't be sure. I don't think I had ever seen her wear makeup.

"We got tickets for you already," Sonya said as she handed them to us. "We better get in there 'cause it looks like seats are pretty sparse."

She was right. There was no spot with enough seats to accommodate all eight of us.

"We're gonna have to split up," Seth whispered. The theatre was getting dark and the previews were about to start. "Every man for himself."

It just worked out that Sonya was right behind me. Jiggle found a seat with Zander and Nabbi, leaving only me and Sonya without a place to sit.

"There are two up there," Sonya whispered in my ear, and pointed to the front row.

I nodded and headed for the two seats. I started to get nervous when I realized what this meant; Sonya and I would be alone among a hundred people for two hours.

It blows to watch a movie in the front row; you have to lean back in your seat and your neck gets cramped staring almost straight up at the screen. I also got a little motion sick from the changing camera angles. But the kink in my neck and the nausea were not the most uncomfortable thing about my seat—I felt like such a tool sitting beside Sonya. Should I make conversation? Should I ignore her? Should I buy us some popcorn?

I must've liked her because I had cotton-mouth and a hundred little beads of sweat formed on my upper lip.

Sonya leaned over to me and whispered, "I'm glad we got to sit together." I could feel the air on my earlobe when she said it.

"Yeah, great seats," I said like an idiot. She shimmied to the edge of her seat and our shoulders were touching. We watched the movie for a while. My eyes stayed locked on the screen, but I hadn't computed one word from the film. All I could think about was the heat from her shoulder on mine. Could she be into me? Me, Brook Gunderson, with the lanky body and middle name Wayburn?

I tried to push the idea out of my head, but then she shifted the position of her hand. She moved it down to her knee, right beside my leg. I could tell it was not the most comfortable place to rest a hand, but she kept it there anyway.

I was panicking, thinking, I guess I have to hold her hand now. She's expecting it. If I don't, she'll think I'm a wuss.

I had a flashback to the last time I held a girl's hand. Grade 5, Megan O'Malley.

Megan and I were "going out." She had her best friend give me a note with hearts all over it and the inscription: *4 your eyes only.* The note asked if I would be Megan's boyfriend. It had three words and a small box beside each, *YES, NO,* or *MAYBE.* I checked the "yes" box and that was the most communicating we did our whole relationship.

So there we were, with eight other elementary school couples, sitting in a circle holding hands in the soccer field. I couldn't look at Megan and she was too shy to look at me. Our hands were starting to sweat, but I just kept squeezing. In Grade 5, Ryan Mitchell and Chelsea Aarons were the popular couple, and the rest of us did whatever they said or did. That day they were saying "Kiss." Chelsea would point to a pair of us and then the whole group would chant "Kiss! Kiss! Kiss!" We were about the sixth group picked. We walked hand in hand to the middle of the circle, the chant echoing from a faraway place. I just closed my eyes and then—*smack*—her cold fish lips were pressed against mine. It was a quick peck, nothing like the soap operas. I thought it was over— we'd paid our dues to fit in—but then the chant switched to "French! French! French!" I didn't know what the heck that meant, but Megan seemed to know. She looked at me with this dreamy look that she probably thought was sexy and leaned in. It looked more like when a chimpanzee is trained to kiss their trainer. It was just a mess of long lips curling and twitching in the air.

It couldn't have lasted more than six seconds, but it ruined me for six years. She actually put her warm, wet tongue in my mouth! The fact that her primary taste organ was intruding on my oral cavity was not the worst part; she was spinning it around like a madman, and deep too, near my tonsils. Our teeth were banging and my tongue was just flopping around for the ride. I swear if I had braces like she did, you could have seen sparks fly.

Near the end of the ordeal, I swear Megan's tongue touched that little hanging-down thing in the back of my throat, and I retched. I didn't full-out puke in her mouth, but a few acrid chunks came up.

I could tell she tasted it 'cause she straightaway unlocked our lips and cried out: "Eew, gross!"

She quickly stalked away, trying to hold back the tears. I just stood there in the middle of the popular kids getting perfect surround-sound of the cackling. One particularly witty fellow yelled out over the ruckus, "Barfing Brook and Gaggin' Megan!"

Let's just say that I received a breakup note (without the hearts or check boxes) in my locker the next day, and I officially resigned from the game of dating . . . I thought for life. I hoped Sonya didn't remember Barfing Brook and Gaggin' Megan.

Sonya's pinkie finger was resting on my knee. Man, you're a moron, I said to myself, just grab her hand, she wants you to! But I couldn't. I told my hand to move, but it wouldn't listen to my brain. I decided to count to three, but on "three" I chickened out again. I did the countdown thing about twenty more times, each time a guilt-ridden failure. The movie was almost over and I hadn't caught a single thing. Each time I talked myself into grabbing her hand, I talked myself out of it with lame excuses like "The mood isn't right in this action sequence" or "This is a romantic part, if I hold her hand now it will be too cheesy."

On the screen, the hero was fighting the final battle—in my head, ditto. I knew the credits were going to roll in a few minutes; I had to suck it up—it was now or never. The fear of Sonya thinking I was a wimp overcame my fear of holding her hand. I just closed my eyes and grabbed. I missed the hand and hit the forearm, but Sonya corrected it, and we interlocked fingers.

"I thought I was going to have to ask you in writing," she said with a smile. I just giggled anxiously. I've had a lot of Pop Rocks in my belly before, but today it was like they were running through my veins—exploding like firecrackers in every capillary. I thought back to the poem about the swooping whirlwind of love. Maybe the poets do know what they're talking about.

When the movie ended, our shoes crunched the popcorn and stuck to the floor as we sidestepped out to the aisle. We decided to break the clasp, even though neither of us spoke. We just understood each other—it might be too early to let the boys know.

"Frazier has committed himself to a rehabilitation clinic," Mum said as she flipped pancakes in the pan. "The money he borrowed from me was to pay for a bus ticket to Edmonton and to be admitted."

She might as well have hit me with the pan; it wouldn't have surprised me more than this news about Fraze. He used to swear that all that therapy mumbo-jumbo is for the *real* sick people, not the ones who could quit if they wanted to. I couldn't tell if she was happy or sad because her face was turned away from me.

"What? You mean he just woke up this morning and decided to enter a program?" I asked, sitting straight up.

"Apparently he decided a while ago, before he came home. I guess you have to wait sometimes before a spot opens up. Nobody knew he was even thinking about it. He just left a note on the counter this morning before Dad left for work saying he was sorry for all the grief he's caused and where he was going." She didn't seem either excited or relieved.

"That's a good thing, right?" I asked.

"It's a great thing." She slapped a pancake on my plate. "If Fraze will go through the whole program, that is. Icing sugar before the big game?"

"No thanks, I'll just eat them plain." I didn't want icing sugar to affect my stamina. I knew I wouldn't be pitching until tomorrow night's game, but I wanted to be prepared for it.

"Your brother is going to need a lot of support over the next few weeks."

"Yeah."

"Maybe you and Jason could drive up and visit him sometime," she suggested.

"Yeah, definitely; for sure," I said. I didn't really mean it though. Not only was it a five-hour drive to Edmonton, but I also hadn't talked about the incident at all with Jiggle. Of course he knew—everyone did—he was just being a good guy and hadn't brought it up. It was so weird, I just didn't want to form any sentences that had to do with it. But most of all, I didn't want to drive all the way to Edmonton to see my big brother shaking in the corner of some bleached white room with a wide-open hospital gown exposing his skinny butt. I would rather visit him in Alcatraz.

I gave my mum a kiss on the cheek for the first time since I was seven and told her that it was going to be okay, Frazier is a tough kid. She smiled and told me she would try to be at all of our games this tournament, camcorder in hand.

I felt good in my freshly washed uniform as I waited on the curb for Jiggle to pick me up. I was back in baseball, about to play in the most important tournament of my life, and Frazier was looking to be on the right path. I smiled and felt the skin stretch around my ears. It had been a while since those muscles had been stretched.

It was the first round, so I would be watching this one. Coach wanted to save me for the second round when we would meet the Bulldogs, if we both won.

Our city was hosting the Provincials, which was bittersweet— bitter because we would not get to go on another road trip, sweet because we had home-field advantage. The south zone had two seeds in the tournament: the Northside Bulldogs and us. The Calgary zone had three representatives, and Edmonton had three, making it an eight-team tournament. According to the ranking system, we were ranked fifth, the Bulldogs second, and the Edmonton team called the Kodiaks, to whom we had already lost, were ranked first.

THE CHARGERS, who were our first-round matchup, were already on the field when Jiggle, Sonya, and I pulled up to the field. Sonya and I were sitting closer than before in the front seat of Jiggle's truck, and she kept finding reasons to reach over and put her hand on my leg, always with a sneaky smile. The Calgary team was doing some semi-erotic partner stretches in the outfield. One guy was flat on his back while another pushed his legs toward his head with both hands. The guy pushing was facing the guy lying on the grass, so his crotch was close to the other guy's butt.

"I think I saw that stretch on the internet," Jiggle joked as we walked away from the parking lot.

"Don't be a perv," Sonya said, and kicked Jiggle's back heel, causing him to trip.

It was a good day for baseball, but then again when isn't it a good day for baseball? The field looked great. They'd brought in professional landscapers for the tournament. I guess Jiggle and I weren't good enough for the Provincial Championships.

After we finished warm-ups, Nabbi and Oberg went to the captains' meeting to call the coin toss. Zander told them that he'd had a dream of a beaver the night before and interpreted it as a message from the baseball gods meaning we should choose tails because the majestic beaver is stamped on the tail side of the Canadian nickel. Oberg called tails and won.

Our captains chose to be the home squad, giving us last at-bats. They went three-up three-down on four pitches. Randall pitched four balls low at the first three batters' knees and all three grounded out. It was the fastest half-inning I had ever seen.

The Chargers' pitcher had some heat, but not a lot of control. He was the type of guy that would make you nervous at the plate 'cause you never knew if it would be a strikeout or a knockout. He walked Charlton in six pitches. Coach is aggressive early in games; he likes to play with a lead. He gave Charlton the steal sign, and on the first pitch, he swiped second easily. Sonya had trouble catching up to this guy and struck out for only the third time this season. I tried to act like I didn't notice.

With Nabbi at the plate, Coach gave the indicator and then slid his finger over the brim of his hat: the sign for the hit-and-run. Charlton took off from second as soon as the pitcher started his windup and Nabbi hit a low fastball like a cricket pitch for a seeing-eye single up the middle. With Charlton's speed and his good jump on the pitch, he scored on a close play at the plate with a beautiful hook slide.

He slid around the catcher, who was kneeling on the third-base line, dragging his back leg behind him. He dove far enough away so that the catcher couldn't reach him with the tag, then at the last second he stretched his back leg out and barely brushed the plate as he slid by. I got goosebumps on my arm when the ump yelled, "Safe." My dream of winning the provincial title seemed closer than ever.

One run was all the scoring until the sixth. Randall had been pitching well and held them to a goose egg on the scoreboard for the first five innings. But in the sixth, they finally got to him, scoring three runs. We were down 3–1 when we came up to bat in the top of the seventh—our last chance. I had a lump in my throat when Coach K. told us that according to the statistics, and our history, we had a 60 percent chance of mounting a comeback.

Sonya squinted toward the mound as she took a few slow swings; the stripe of black makeup under her eyes wasn't lessening the glare from the setting sun. The third baseman was playing deep; he obviously hadn't scouted Sonya well enough. When Sonya noticed him playing back behind the bag, she dragged a perfect bunt down the third-base line that died in the infield grass. By the time the third baseman bare-handed it, Sonya was almost on first base; he held on to the throw, not wanting to risk an error.

Nabbi, who had a .389 batting average this year, stepped to the plate next, and ripped the first fastball he saw. Unfortunately, the second baseman didn't have to move an inch to catch the line drive. One out. When Oberg spat a stream of black liquorice juice (which he thinks makes him look more like a major leaguer chewing tobacco) over the plate preparing for his at-bat, we all had our rally caps on, facing Yankee Stadium. We were praying for his tenth dinger of the season to tie the score. However, the Chargers had done their homework on Shane Oberg. The catcher stood up with his glove held to the side and they intentionally walked our cleanup hitter. There were a few boos from the crowd as he trotted to first.

With runners on second and first, the announcer said, "Now up for the Mustangs, the first baseman, Jason Parker." Jiggle-Me Jason stepped to the plate and stared down the pitcher, looking like a young Cecil Fielder. The first pitch was a called-strike curveball. The next two pitches were in the dirt. Two and one. Jiggle, eager to hit something hard, took a huge swing at the next fastball and missed pretty bad. If I was pitching, I'd feed him a steady diet of four-seamers after that display. The pitcher had the same idea and reached back to blow a fastball by Jiggle. The pitch was right down the pipe and Jiggle took his characteristic huge swing, but this time the ball hit the meat of the bat and jumped high and deep toward left field. Everyone on both benches, and in the crowd, jumped to their feet to get a better look at the ball soaring out toward the wall. A slight breeze picked up and pushed Jiggle's blast back a few feet. The left fielder got under the falling ball and set up to jump, but he timed it poorly, and the ball cleared the fence by a foot. The whole bench was jumping up and down, knocking over bats, equipment, and the tub of water. Jiggle jogged around first base with a huge grin on his face. The jog turned into a cowboy smacking his horse on its rump as Jiggle trotted around second and third. His first home run of the season warranted a little showboating. We mobbed him at the plate, smacking his helmet and jumping up and down in a synchronized bounce of a dozen people.

We won the game 4–3. Jiggle was the hero, and I felt happy for him. In the locker room after the game, Jiggle was replaying the story over and over again to anyone who would listen, and the ball got hit farther and farther each time he told it.

I let him tell me about the pitch a few times on the way home in his truck. I even ignored that he said it was a full count when I knew it really was only two and two; a full count is more dramatic.

When he didn't turn down my street, I said, "Where we going? I can't go out tonight—we have the biggest game of our lives tomorrow."

"We just have one little thing to do, it shouldn't take long."

I recognized the look in my best friend's eye—there was something up.

"No way, man. I can't risk any more trouble this close to the final. Coach finally doesn't hate me."

"We're playing the Bulldogs tomorrow, dude. We can't just stand by and do nothing to them," Jiggle said.

I WAITED IN THE TRUCK as Jiggle went to check out the security situation at Northside High. Beside me was an ice-cream bucket full to the brim with powdered laundry soap that had been saturated with liquid dish soap and red food colouring. Jiggle and I were wearing all black and he had some pantyhose over his head that squished his nose. When he told me it was all clear, I pulled the pantyhose over my head and carried the soap bucket toward the school courtyard.

Built in the middle of the courtyard is the hallowed Northside High fountain. It's just a small pool surrounding a stone tree with a spout coming out of the top. The tree is supposed to represent the Tree of Knowledge, and the water is learning that constantly flows from its branches.

Jiggle grabbed the bucket of soap and poured it down the tree-spout. Because the water was just recycled from the pool below, the soap started to bubble everywhere. The bubbles were supposed to be red, like our school colours, but they turned out pink. I guess we should have thought of that, but the Bulldogs would get the message. We admired the billowing pink tide for a minute or two until the suds started to overflow from the pool and onto the concrete ground, creeping toward our shoes.

"That is going to be awesome by tomorrow morning!" Jiggle was laughing as we skipped back to the truck.

"Let's come back in the morning to check it out," I suggested. "We can go incognito."

THE NEXT MORNING we parked a few blocks away from the school. We walked toward the courtyard with our hats pulled low over our eyes to hide our identities. It looked like there was an exam, because a bunch of students were headed the same way. Thankfully, we didn't have an exam until tomorrow.

The courtyard was a two-foot-deep pool of pink bubbles, glittering in the sun. Some people thought it was a riot and were sliding and playing in the suds, trying to get their friends wet.

The French teacher balanced on the edge of the pool, not wanting to wreck his pointy leather shoes, on his way to the doorway. "*Mesdames et messieurs*, please clear zee path to zee doorway, *s'il vous plaît.*" I could tell he was a little ticked off because he kept mumbling things to himself in French as he tried to hold his pinstriped pant legs up and balance his latte at the same time. "*Merde!*" he cussed as he slipped and almost lost his balance.

A couple of people spied Jiggle and me laughing our faces off and pointed in our direction. We decided this was our cue to exit, and speed-walked back to the truck. Jiggle was of course exaggerating the speed walk swing-of-the-hips, looking like one of those walking marathoners.

The rest of the day, I sat in my room visualizing each pitch I would throw. I read in a magazine once that a guy in a concentration camp stayed sane for three years by playing a round of golf in his head every day. When he came out, he had shaved ten strokes off his handicap, just by visualization. I was visualizing striking out Luke Fabro.

Fifteen

CIRCUS CATCH—A spectacular catch, suggesting the moves of a circus acrobat.

Frazier's therapist called from Edmonton. I guess when you're in rehab they try to remove the toxins from your head as well as your body. The therapist said that we should all write Frazier a note of encouragement. She told us that if the family acknowledged Frazier's effort and provided support, Fraze would be more likely to succeed in the program. I had no idea what the program was, nor did I know how to write a note of encouragement. It seemed to me about as awkward as a pig on roller skates. I don't know how to write; I was hardly passing high school English. I especially don't know how to express my feelings to my big brother. The closest I had come to telling him I care about him was when I bought him a snow cone at the ball diamond when he was out of cash, and that was way before the weirdness set in between us. I didn't have time for fluffy "I love you" notes anyway. Today was the provincial semifinal.

THIS GAME IS HUGE, I thought, as I sat at the end of the dugout and tied the double knot in my left cleat. Next, I pulled my hat down and curved the brim around my eyes. If we won, we'd be in the finals. If we lost, we were done.

"Brook, we're going to start you tonight," Coach K. said. His magnified eyes looked shifty behind his thick glasses. "But I don't want you to throw a single knuckleball until the first batter. Just warm up like you'll be pitching the fastball again."

"I'll try, Coach, but I want to practise the knuckler a bit. Make sure it's working."

"The surprise will be worth it," he assured me. "Sixty percent of teams take three or more innings to rebound from a surprise like that."

I just nodded and said, "Okay." Coach could be weird sometimes, but he really wanted this game bad.

The captains called tails again at the coin toss, and they were right, again. We chose to be home team, meaning I took the mound first. Seven innings to immortality on the Wall of Champions.

There was a bag of rosin behind the rubber. You move it around in your hand and the powder absorbs any moisture you have on it. We never had one before, but this was the big time—the Provincials. I only threw twenty pitches in the bullpen, but my palms and pits were soaking. I bounced the rosin bag a few times in my hand, sending a cloud up around me.

The first inning was about to start but there was no Zander. I was just standing on the mound with nobody to throw to. Behind the dugout I saw him, dressed in full equipment, brushing his teeth. He leaned over and spat the toothpaste froth into the grass just feet away from the concession stand. A little girl holding a Popsicle started to cry when some splattered on her shoes.

"Zander! Let's go, pal," I yelled across the infield.

He ran toward me, carrying his helmet awkwardly under his arm. "Sorry, Brook. I play better with clean teeth."

"Just get back there. I want at *least* two warm-up pitches," I said.

I tried to throw a good, hard fastball, but it looked more like a softball change-up. I tried again, but I had to arch it to get it all the way to the plate.

"It looks like we're facing Princess Brook tonight, boys," a voice echoed from inside the other team's brick dugout. "Watch out for that fastball, the sun might go down by the time it gets to the plate."

I didn't even have to look to know who it was. Luke Fabro was posing like a male model with his bat forming a T on his shoulders, his arms draped over each end. I looked through him toward the bleachers, adjusted my cup, and spat in his direction. When I looked at that guy, I could feel my blood boiling.

The first batter dug into the box, and a shiver surged up my core. I couldn't wait to show these guys the new Gunner. I dug my vampire nails into the stitches of the new baseball, balancing it gingerly on my thumb. The first pitch I threw glided toward the plate, appearing motionless. The batter's eyes became huge, like he was going to hit it out of the park, and missed it by ten inches. A hush came over their dugout; the chatter from their bench turned to silence. I could feel their shock. Nobody in our league had ever used a knuckleball effectively. Even the ump took his glasses off and wiped them in amazement.

The next two pitches floated like the first and I recorded the first strikeout of my comeback. The batter shook his head in disbelief as he headed back to the Bulldogs' bench. My heart was pounding and I could hardly stop the smile from breaking through. I never felt this happy on the mound, not even when I had my fastball.

The next hitter swung weakly at the first pitch, and hit a soft grounder to Sonya, who side-armed it to Jiggle for the second out.

The third hitter was also their pitcher, and my nemesis, Luke Fabro. I had been waiting to face this guy since I pegged him in the neck. I bet I would have struck him out if I hadn't had to bean him.

Fabro had had a great season; he led the league in batting average at .435 and was second to Oberg in round-trippers. Fabro watched the first one go by, with a smirk on his overly symmetrical face. When I let go of the next one, I felt one of my fingers extend too fast. The ball flew toward home plate spinning more than I wanted it to. Fabro made no mistake and crushed the lame duck into the gap in left centre. When he was on second with a stand-up double, he called "Time" and took off his helmet, revealing his golden mane. He made sure the crowd could see him preening on second base before brushing his hair back and putting his helmet back on. His arms were flexed the whole time.

With two out, their cleanup hitter was way overzealous. He tried to hit each of my offerings out of the park and ended up hitting a routine pop fly out to Charlton in centre field. Not a bad inning of work, I thought, as I jogged to the dugout, being careful to jump over the foul line on the way there.

Fabro was really mowing us down with the fastball. The umpire seemed to concur because he kept on starting the lawn mower after each strikeout. After two innings, the score was zeros, and he had struck out five. Sonya was the only one who hit it into play, but it was a ground ball to the first baseman.

I was hitting in the nine spot, so I didn't face Fabro until the bottom of the third. I came up with two out; I was the only chance to end the no-hitter. I stepped into the box and went through my routine. Tap both edges of the plate with the bat, dig in my back foot, and take two practice swings. Fabro was pitching from the full windup and the first pitch was a fastball up and in. I should have known, considering our relationship. The ball came hurtling toward my head so fast I could hear it whistling. I hit the dirt, landing on my back, my bat flying behind me like a misguided helicopter propeller. I was a victim of a "brushback" pitch. The umpire instantly darted to the mound to give Fabro a warning. He knew our history and said that if Fabro tried that again he would be suspended from high school baseball for life. Fabro just smiled over the ump's shoulder at me like poison come to dinner.

I dusted myself off and got ready for the next pitch. I was waiting on a fastball, since no one had touched it yet. When it came, I was ready; I swung and made good contact in the middle of the barrel. I was way behind it, but it soared just over the first baseman's extended glove and into right field. I settled for a single, not wanting to push my luck. That hit moved me up to a .268 batting average for the year. Not too shabby, I thought as I put my batting gloves into my back pocket, making a ball-shaped lump.

In the fourth inning, the score was still 0–0, and I was getting worried about our chances. Fabro had been unhittable, and I was starting to doubt that my knuckles could keep the strong offence of the Bulldogs off the board.

My doubts turned into reality. The sun had been beating down on me all evening and the fatigue contributed to a lack of concentration. When you only throw fastballs, you can let your brain shut off and just go into a trance. With the knuckleball, you have to keep your head in the game every pitch. The Bulldogs put together a string of hits on a few pitching mistakes and went up 2–0. Fabro continued to keep us scoreless in the bottom of the fourth, and we were looking at only two innings to mount a comeback.

In the fifth inning, I gave up a hit to their lead-off man, and I cursed under my breath. I was in a bit of a jam. Coach called a time out and visited me on the mound.

"I'm not going to take you out" was the first thing he said to me. "Randall just cut the cheese in the dugout and I needed to get the heck outta there," he said. Coach actually made a joke. It almost seemed as if he liked me. "No pressure, Gunner. There are 1.4 billion people in China that don't even know this game is going on."

"Thanks, Coach," I said. "I just need to concentrate on my pitch."

"All right then, let's do it." He put the ball in my mitt and patted me on the butt. Baseball is the only game where grown men can pat underage boys on the rump without causing a lawsuit.

Our talk settled me down a little and I floated three pitches by the next batter. He fouled one off but missed two for my second strikeout of the game.

Pitching from the stretch, I kept an eye on the runner on first base. He was more of a threat to steal because of how slow my knuckleball was. I checked him once more and then sent the pitch that rotated slowly and glided low and outside. The batter hit it hard to Nabbi at short, who flipped it underhand to Sonya, who wheeled and fired to Jiggle, jumping over the runner as he slid spikes up at her legs, and completed the twin-killing. A beautiful play and, man, she looked cute with her hair tucked behind her ears under her hat.

We caught a big break in the sixth inning. The Bulldogs took Fabro out with the two-run lead. They wanted to save his arm for the final game they expected to play in. This did two things. First, it whizzed everyone off that they were so cocky. Second, it gave us an opportunity to hit against their number two pitcher.

The new guy was Gwinn Dumont, the third baseman whose name I use as an alias when I get in trouble. He had a good arm, but wasn't nearly as dominating as Fabro. We had the top of the order up for us, and Charlton led off with a ground ball deep in the hole that the shortstop picked up, but couldn't throw in time to get the speedster. Coach wanted to play small-ball, so he signalled for the sacrifice bunt. Sonya executed it perfectly, sending a roller down toward first base. Charlton slid into second, while the first baseman put a swinging tag on Sonya that almost knocked her to the ground.

"That's freakin' bush-league!" I yelled out. I wanted to jump on the guy and break his nose, but Jiggle and Oberg held me back. "That's pretty tough, picking on a five-foot-two, ninety-pound girl, ya dog dink!" I was in that mode again where I don't think before I speak.

"I'm a hundred and four pounds, I'll have you know," Sonya said. "Besides that guy hits like my sister." Nothing is a big deal to Sonya.

The crowd was arguing in the bleachers—Randall's dad told a Northside dad where to go and how to get there—and it took the umpires a few minutes before they got control again. When they did, we had a runner on second, one out, and Nabbi Ghedi at the plate. He got a nice fastball over the heart of the plate that he knocked high in the air toward the gap in right centre. The centre fielder had a good jump on the ball and made a game-saving catch on the run. Two out, down by two.

Our best RBI man, Shane Oberg, stepped to the plate. If he finds a piece of grass, we score a run. Oberg let the first three pitches go by for balls. Dumont didn't want to risk anything over the middle of the plate to the slugger. With three balls and no strikes, everyone in the park expected the take to be on—that Oberg would let the next pitch go by, but Coach K. gave the "swing away" sign from his spot beside third base. The pitch was a fat fastball right down the heart of the plate. Oberg leaned into it, and we heard that sweet sound of aluminum on rawhide. The whole place knew it was gone as soon as he hit it. The ball soared like a bullet over the scoreboard and landed thirty feet in the tennis court behind the park. It was a monster shot that tied the game at two.

Jiggle, being so excited from Oberg's dinger, almost went back-to-back with a long blast to left. Unfortunately, the fielder made a great catch at the wall and ended the inning.

So with the game tied, we went into the last inning. It was like I was living in a baseball movie. My knees were shaking as I thought about stepping on the mound for the seventh time that night, and maybe the last time that season. I repeated the knuckle-ball instructions from the internet as I walked to the mound—it had become my mantra. My arm felt heavy in the socket and I wished I hadn't thrown so much against the mattress during the week.

The first pitch fluttered by the hitter for strike one. I felt a solitary drop of sweat fall from my armpit into my lucky Red Sox undershirt. He connected with the next pitch and it one-hopped up to me. I took my time—pounding the ball into the pocket a few times—then threw it hard to Jiggle at first. One out.

I worked the next batter to a full count; my breaths were shallow, like when you are at a high altitude, as I delivered the 3–2 pitch. I walked the bum, when ball four floated high and outside.

I could feel my control deteriorating. The next batter hit a routine ground ball to Randall at third. He made the play, but seeing how fast the hitter was accelerating toward first, he rushed and lost the grip on the ball. When he found the handle again, he rifled it to Jiggle—I knew it would be a close play. Jiggle, surprisingly flexible for a big man, stretched out toward the ball almost into the splits, thus shortening the distance of the throw by one foot. The ball snapped into his glove, like a popped balloon. The first base umpire, who was kneeling on one knee to get a better look, hesitated as if replaying the scene in his mind, then erupted with a "You're outta there!" punching the air as he yelled.

With two out and one on second, you could feel the tension of both teams. No one was talking, and a few of the Bulldogs were holding hands in their dugout.

The fourth batter of the inning hit a line drive into right field. Seth broke toward the screaming leather without the typical fear in his eyes. Before the ball hit the ground, he slid, allowing his precious glove to drag in the dirt, and found the baseball. It barely balanced on the top of his glove, half in the mitt, half out, like a snow cone as he tumbled to a halt. Thankfully, he controlled the circus catch to save a run, and our season.

"Attaboy, Southpaw!" I yelled to Seth as he wiped his mitt off and grinned at being called his nickname for the first time. I could've kissed him, I was so happy.

It was the bottom of the seventh. Tie game. Zander called an emergency meeting before we got ready to bat.

"I know this sounds crazy, but we all have to drink out of this," he said, holding an empty plastic athletic supporter full of water in his hands like a peasant bringing forth gifts to a king.

"That is freakin' nasty!" Seth scoffed while looking down at the jockstrap.

"It's been thoroughly cleaned," Zander assured us, matter-of-factly. "It belonged to Nate Baines, one of the players who played in the provincial title in '78. I promise you it will sway the baseball gods in our favour."

"Give it here," I told Zander, and guzzled the whole thing. It didn't taste bad, but it didn't taste good either. I would have done anything to win the game. A few of the others took small sips from the holy jock, cringing as it went down.

It looked like the gods approved of the "swigging of the jock" ritual because the Bulldogs made two errors and gave up a walk to load the bases. I came up smack in the middle of every baseball player's childhood fantasy. It was the bottom of the last inning, bases loaded, tie game. I noticed that I had chewed my nails on my non-pitching hand down to the skin and they were stinging.

I took a few practice swings while Coach told me to be patient, "even a little fly ball to the outfield will win us the game."

I drifted back to the time Jiggle and I were hitting golf balls off the hill into the river bottom; how I pretended I was in this moment, and on the hill, I knocked in the winning run. I could use a 500-foot grand slam right now.

"You playing here, number eleven?" The umpire snapped me back to reality.

I can do this, I told myself as I went through my routine for the fourth time tonight. Be aggressive, he has to throw strikes to you. If he walks you, then the winning run is forced home and their season is ruined. You control this situation. Wait for your pitch.

The pitcher brought the fastball to start out with; I took a swing at it and fouled it off. Next one was a curveball; I watched it for strike two. I was in a hole. Next, he tried an outside fastball that

I took a check swing at, but thankfully the umpire said I didn't go around. The count was two strikes and one ball. I stepped out of the box to dry my hands and think it over. This is a pitcher's count. He might try to make me chase something out of the zone. I stepped back in, deciding I was going to be aggressive and go for the next pitch if it was anywhere close.

Dumont wiped the sweat from his brow, checked the loaded bases one runner at a time, and started his windup. I concentrated on the ball in his hand; from here I could see the veins in his forearm as he started to snap his wrist. The ball spun out of his hand, coming toward me at seventy miles per hour, but I had time to think. Time slowed down. It was a fastball, inside, chest high, maybe a strike. The red seams blended with the white leather to make a pink orb, almost here. I knew what I needed to do. I leaned my shoulder a little bit forward and squeezed the bat, preparing for the pitch. All I heard was a loud crack.

MAN, WHAT IS stinging my nose? I thought through the fog that had invaded my brain. My eyes slowly opened to see Coach K. waving a little vial with yellow grains in it.

"That stuff reeks," I said between coughs.

"It's smelling salts, Brook. You were unconscious."

I guess when I allowed the pitch to hit me, it pinched a nerve on my spine, causing me to pass out. The ambulance came through an opening in the centre field fence and drove right through the infield, stopping beside me as I lay in the dirt. I was grateful that it didn't drive over the mound—that would be sacrilegious. I could feel my legs and arms, so I didn't think it was too serious, but my mum and dad, who were pretty frantic, insisted that I go to the hospital.

My neck was immobilized and my forehead strapped down as the paramedics lifted me into the back of the ambulance. I couldn't see much, but I was able to see my whole team standing in a row beside the dugout clapping furiously for me. Even Oberg had a smile on his face that seemed to say "Good job." Coach K. helped lift the body plank and before the door shut he whispered, only loud enough that I could hear, "That was the most unselfish thing I have ever seen anybody do in sports. I'm proud to have you on my team." Then the doors slammed shut.

"We won, right?" I asked my mum, in the back of the ambulance as we sped to the hospital.

"Yes, Brook. You beat the Northside Bulldogs, 3–2."

That statement felt better than any amount of morphine they could inject into me. I lay back and enjoyed the ride to the emergency room, wishing I could have seen old Fabro's reaction as the last run was forced around because I jumped in front of an inside fastball.

Sixteen

CHIN MUSIC—A beanball or knockdown pitch that passes close to the batter's jaw. Also known as a brushback or "close shave" used to intimidate opposing batters.

In the picture taken for the Wall of Champions at school, Oberg and Seth had their arms folded and were pushing their biceps out with their fists, trying to look ripped. I gave it a shot, but my chicken arms looked too weird with a bulge.

I had missed the final game of the season because Dr. Gunderson wouldn't permit me to play with minor sensation deficits in my toes. It wouldn't have mattered anyway; the Kodiaks handled the rest of the boys pretty easily, winning 7–2. However, today we were all smiles, and not just because we wanted to look good for the photo shoot. Second place in the province wasn't too shabby. We *were* the best Westside High baseball team in almost thirty years, but the way we were whooping it up, you might have thought we'd won the National League Pennant—after all, we did beat the Bulldogs! After the photo shoot, most of the team came over to my place to watch the tape of the semifinal game that my mum recorded.

"If you listen closely, you can hear Brook's knuckleball giggle as it goes past the batter," Zander joked.

"I think that was Sonya giggling at Brook's tight pants," Jiggle piped up.

Sonya and I were holding hands on the couch, interlocked fingers and everything. I didn't care if the team knew. In fact, I wanted them to know. I wanted everyone to know.

We watched a few innings, making fun of Luke Fabro's hair, and Zander brushing his teeth before every inning. Then, when I got beaned in the last inning, the tape got all crazy as my mum screamed. The next half-hour was footage of an empty pop can that somebody discarded on the bleachers. Mum forgot to turn off the tape when she put the recorder down.

With the empty pop can the only footage to occupy our minds, Seth thought it would be a great opportunity to retell the story of his snow-cone catch for about the twentieth time.

Just as he got the story started with "Before the seventh inning, I just had this feeling that they would hit it out to right field, so I prepared myself," Jiggle cut him off with "You better prepare yourself for an atomic, gonch-pulled-right-over-your-head-and-hooked-on-your-upper-lip-wedgie if you think we are gonna listen to that story one more time, Seth."

"Yeah, that story *is* getting a tad old there, Seth. Not that it wasn't a good catch, buddy," Sonya said.

Seth looked a little offended at Jiggle, but not at Sonya.

"Hey, why don't we play some Whiffleball in the backyard, guys?" I suggested, to defuse any argument that might boil up.

We had played a lot of Whiff in the backyard before high school and had a ton of fun. Something about holding that skinny, yellow plastic bat always sent me back to a happy time.

"Sure! I get first ups," Oberg said, jumping off the couch.

The sun was still shining and an easy breeze blew through the neighbour's fence as I threw the plastic ball to Oberg. It was a great day for baseball. But what day isn't?

Mum's guest mattress, brown and a little mouldy smelling, served as a catcher and home plate. The rest of the team stood around the backyard, waiting for the ball to come their way.

After Oberg hit, Jiggle-Me Jason grabbed the bat.

"Okay, who am I?" he asked. Then, as the plastic ball came toward him, he turned his back to it and let it hit him. He let out a girlish yelp, and like a movie starlet from the twenties, placed the back of his hand to his forehead, did a pirouette, and mimed an elaborate fainting routine.

"Real funny, pal," I said, as Jiggle lay in the grass still pretending he was unconscious. I picked up the ball and whipped it at him, but missed because I was still kind of laughing.

Just then, I heard my mum call down from the porch to me, "Brook, could you come in for a second? There's a man here to see you."

When I looked up at her, she had a strange, expressionless look on her face. I wondered what was going on. Then she noticed the mattress.

"Brook Wayburn Gunderson! Is that the mattress from the guest room?"

"That old thing? I'm not totally sure to be honest," I said, dishonestly.

"Come inside this instant, young man," she said.

"See ya later, Wayburn," Jiggle said, putting the emphasis on "Wayburn" as I walked up the steps.

When I walked into the house, I was surprised to see a large man in a dark suit sitting in the front room with my father.

They both stood up as I entered the room.

"You must be Brook Gunderson," the man in the suit said.

"Um . . . " Looking at this guy with the large jaw and sunglasses in his suit pocket, I was sure he was a cop or detective or something. I thought of all the laws I had broken in the last few months. The golf balls? The Hamilton Hop? The lawn mowing? The mannequin? The fountain? Crap, I'm busted. This guy is going to haul me off to juvenile court and I'm gonna have to live in a group home and clean up highways in an orange jumpsuit.

"I'm Dalton Jones from the University of Texas. I was wondering if I could talk to you about that game you pitched the other day."

I was flabbergasted. I didn't know what to say. "Er er" was all I could manage.

I turned back to Mum, who was smiling as she slipped into the room behind me. The large Mr. Jones sat on one couch, and the three of us sat opposite, squished together on the other.

"As I told your parents, I'm an athletic director at the University of Texas. I was up here in Canada visiting my mother. I decided to catch a ball game and I saw you pitch. That knuckleball you throw is pretty impressive."

"Well, I'm just using it until my arm strength comes back. I'm actually a fastballer . . . I had an injury this year."

"Oh yeah? Other than taking one for the team in the middle of the back?" he joked.

"That was just a stinger. A few months back, I tore some ligaments in my pitching arm," I said, rubbing my shoulder.

"Hmm." Mr. Jones seemed like he was looking into a far-off place as he paused for a few seconds to scratch his large jaw.

"That was a gutsy play you made at the end of the game," he finally said.

"Oh thanks," I said, embarrassed by the compliment.

"That might have impressed me more than the pitching. That's why I decided to look you up."

I just nodded a few times—I didn't know what to say to that.

"Yup. There are only three things a guy can do when the pitcher throws him some chin music. He can let it intimidate him, and make him a weak hitter. He can dust himself off and get ready for the next pitch. Or he can do what you did and turn the beanball into a run."

As Dalton Jones spoke, I looked over at Mum. She had her eyes fixed on something behind Mr. Jones. It was a picture of the family at the lake before Frazier went away to college. Frazier is balancing Taylor on his shoulders and wearing her water-wings on his wrists, my hat is pulled too low to see my eyes, but my smile fills what is left of my face, and Mum and Dad are holding hands squinting into the sun.

Mum glanced at me through glassy eyes and gave me a small smile, the first I had seen in months. Somehow, I felt like Mr. Jones was talking about more than just baseball.

"Well, we're very proud of how Brook has rebounded from his stint of bad luck with the injury this year," Dad said.

"How hard did you used to throw, son?" Mr. Jones said, pulling me away from my thoughts.

"About eighty to eighty-five" I replied, stretching the truth a smidge.

"I'm going to give you a word of advice if I can," Mr. Jones said to me. "At my school, we trade guys who throw in the low eighties for ice packs and grass fertilizer. We get sixty that try out every year. You stick with that knuckler of yours and you could go places."

"Really?" I said. My voice cracked like a preteen as the word came out.

"Sure. Why, did you know there are only two theories on how to hit a knuckleball?"

"Only two, eh?"

"Yup, and neither of them works."

The Texan laughed heartily at his own joke. I laughed just because I was feeling so good it gave me a chance to get rid of some of the glee that was oozing out.

"Here's my card. I want you to keep working on that papillon of yours, and film the rest of your games. When you're a senior, give me a call and we'll give you a tryout with the team."

"You mean to play baseball in college?" my mum asked.

"Sure. If your son works hard next season, I could see him getting a scholarship to our university."

I could feel my smile stretching the skin by my ears as my mum gave me a side-hug on the couch.

"I have one question Mr. Jones," Dad said, sounding serious. "Will Brook be required to achieve a certain grade point average to be eligible for a scholarship?"

"Yes. All our student-athletes are students first, and athletes second. We don't allow our players to scrape by," he replied.

"Even in English?" Dad said, elbowing me playfully in the ribs.

"Especially in English," Dalton Jones said, winking at my dad.

"I'll study all the poetry of friggin' J. K. Rowling if it means I can play ball," I blurted out.

"I don't think J. K. Rowling writes poetry, Brook," Mum said. Then she looked at Dalton Jones. "I'm sorry. I haven't offered you anything to drink. Would you like some coffee? Tea? Brook can make some lemonade."

"Actually, a glass of that lemonade would sure hit the spot right now, if it's not too much trouble."

"Brook, make some lemonade for Mr. Jones, would you," Dad said.

I put Mr. Jones's card, which I had been thumbing since he gave it to me, into my pocket as I went to make the drinks. As I was stirring the juice I started thinking about everything that had happened this year: the injury, Sonya, the beanball.

I looked out the window at my friends as they continued to play Whiffleball, oblivious to this amazing chain of events. The sun reflected off Sonya's black hair as she squinted her eyes and laughed at Jiggle, who was lying on Seth—playing dead—while Seth struggled like a fish caught in a net to squirm out from under him.

Life was good.

I had just received the greatest news of my young life—that I might still play college baseball, even with a bummed arm, and Frazier was in Edmonton dusting himself off and getting back in the batter's box at the rehab clinic.

Yup, things were more than good.

When the lemonade was mixed, I went to grab a few glasses to drink from. There, below the cupboard, I noticed an envelope. It was covered in stickers and drawings of rainbows and ponies, addressed to Frazier. I had forgotten the letter that the therapist asked us to write.

I brought the lemonade into the front room and poured three glasses. My parents and Mr. Jones were in a riveting conversation about the science behind the southern Alberta chinook.

It seemed like my portion of the conversation was over so I asked, "Would it be all right if told a few people about the good news?"

"That would be fine, Brook," Mr. Jones said. Then he stood up and shook my hand and said, "Remember what I said. Work hard next year on that knuckler, and keep those grades up and I may see you in Texas in a couple of years."

I thanked him for coming and promised to work hard in both baseball and school, then walked back into the kitchen.

I thought about joining my gang in the backyard, but decided against it. Instead, I pulled out a pad of paper and collected my thoughts. I had something I wanted to tell Frazier.

Acknowledgements

I would like to thank: My boys, The Young Toques, without whom many of the sporting and life adventures contained in this book would not have been possible or even conceived. Specifically, I would like to acknowledge Shane Johnson, Darren Majeran, Tyson Smith, David Low, Evan Walters, Conner Hendry, Austin Hornberger, and Nicolas Swagar for providing the inspiration. My editor, Helen Reeves, for moulding the creative process and directing my attention to the areas that needed fleshing out. Kalpna Patel, who plucked the manuscript from among the slush and heartily campaigned on my behalf. Heanok Golom, for his timely critiques. My wife, Erinn, for supporting me during the many hours I chased my pipedream when I should have been studying for medical school.